MW00912921

CONJURES

Book Two of the Tempest Trinity Trilogy

LESLIE CALDERONI

Copyright © 2016 by Leslie Calderoni

All rights reserved

For information about permissions to reproduce selections from this book, translation rights, or to order bulk purchases, write to LC@lesliecalderoni.com.

Cover by Lindsay Gatz at vonRocko Design
Author photo by Jesse Gabriel Photography

Calderoni, Leslie
Conjures: Book two of the Tempest Trinity trilogy
ISBN 978-0-9967046-2-5

1. Young Adult Fiction—Girls & Women. 2. Young Adult Fiction—Science & Technology. 3. Young Adult Fiction—Family / Siblings. 4. Young Adult Fiction— Social Themes / Self-Esteem & Self-Reliance.

Summary: Three gifted teenage sisters must use their powers over the laws of physics to solve a web of mysteries that threatens to tear their family apart.

lesliecalderoni.com
tempesttrinity.com

CONJURES

For Gabriel

"And above all, watch with glittering eyes the whole world around you because the greatest secrets are always hidden in the most unlikely places."

—Roald Dahl

CHAPTER
1

FOR MOST OF MY FIFTEEN YEARS, I've lived a comfortable lie, insulated and clueless. I don't remember a time that I knew Eva as anything other than our aunt.

The moment Mama dropped her truth bomb, my stomach went into freefall. Reality crumbled away like an avalanche; what had seemed stable the moment before came tumbling down, unstoppable, destroying everything in its path. My sisters and I had to pick through the wreckage of memory and emotion to decide what was salvageable.

After the twins and I got our heads around the fact that Auntie Eva was our mother, and Mama our grandmother, each of us handled the new "normal" in her own way.

I chose to forgive them both in spite of the deception, but made it clear to Aracelia that she and Eva own the entire mess. The consequences are theirs to sort through—once we find Eva, that is.

Mia, however, lost her temper completely. I'd never seen her so angry. When I first told the twins the truth, with Mama sitting across from them, staring down at the floor, Mia didn't say a word. Her eyes narrowed and she looked from me to Mama, then back to me. She stood up, pushed her chair in, and walked out of the kitchen. No words—just heat, a sense of betrayal, and the resolve to build a solid brick wall between herself and Mama.

Terra immediately burst into tears and got up right away to hug Mama. All she could get out were the words, "How sad for you. I'm so sorry." Terra's empathy was the salve Mama needed to ease the sting of Mia's anger.

Waiting until fall break to begin our search for Eva—and that mysterious book—turned out not to be as difficult as I'd imagined it would. When Mia wasn't at school or work, she was at Mr. Seville's office answering the phone and prepping legal files. Terra spent her free time following Mama around the house, helping her with chores, and taking every chance to make her laugh. Terra blossoms when she's needed, and Mama's jangled nerves benefited from the soft, warm vibration her granddaughter offered.

I've spent the weeks studying, serving candy to the dwindling crowds of tourists, and poring through the books in Mr. McHenry's library. The weather has turned cooler in the evenings; drizzle streaks the window of my book-lined sanctuary. I keep a fire burning in the brick fireplace most nights while curled up under a warm blanket, sipping chai and losing myself in books about time and relativity.

When the day comes for us to leave for New Orleans, Cheddar shows up at our door two hours early to drive us all to the airport. While Mama's willing to send us to Louisiana, she's not about to let us go without Cheddar. Still in my robe, and my hair in a towel, I meet him at the back door. To his credit, he has a tray of steamy lattes.

"You are a kind and generous boy," I whisper after taking the first sip—a perfect balance of milk, honey, and coffee.

"You nervous about flying?" he asks as he lifts the lid on a frying pan to see what Mama's made us for breakfast.

I can't seem to call her grandma, or *abuela*. She'll always be Mama to me, and Terra feels the same way. But Mia only calls her Aracelia now. When she started, I told her it was disrespectful to the woman who raised us; she said it was disrespectful of *A-ra-ceeeelia* to keep us in the dark, and I didn't have an answer for that, so I dropped it and now that's what she calls her.

"Nervous? No—but you are," I say, gesturing across the table to Cheddar with my latte hand. "You didn't have to come for at least another two hours. However, I forgive you because you brought an offering of caffeine."

"I'm not nervous," he says, indignant. "I'm hungry. Do you mind if I start eating?" Clearly the fear of flying is no match for Cheddar's stomach.

He's on his second helping of chilaquiles when Mia and Terra join us. "Ooh, that looks good!" Terra exclaims, and passes by Cheddar to grab a plate.

"It is," he tries to say through a mouthful of food.

Almost choking, he remembers to chew and swallow. "Aren't you going to eat? It's a long flight from San Jose to New Orleans."

Mia glances at Cheddar's plate and, determining it was Mama who cooked it, wrinkles her nose. "I'll pass."

Cheddar leans back in his chair. "Come on, it's been weeks. You've got to give your grandmother a break eventually."

When I first told Cheddar the news, he was surprised but impressed that they'd pulled off the charade for so long. I warned him not to show his appreciation of the hoax in front of Mia. She's having none of it; reconciliation is not on her agenda. The fact that she's still living under the same roof as Aracelia has more to do with the size of the house than her willingness to move past the issue.

"I'm going to finish packing. I'll meet you guys out front when it's time to go," Mia says quietly as she takes her coffee and leaves the kitchen.

"So glad that wasn't awkward," Cheddar announces as he pushes away from the table.

"She's heartbroken," Terra says softly, using her fork to nudge food around on her plate. "She acts angry to protect herself, but inside she hurts. I try to help, but she always catches on."

"Fourteen years of deception isn't going to resolve itself in a few months," I offer.

"But life is so short," Terra says as she takes her plate to the sink. The way she says it makes me wonder if she feels more than she's admitting.

But time is also short, and we have a plane to catch. We leave Cheddar to clean up the rest of the dishes, securing his place in Mama's good graces.

Upstairs, the chaos is in full swing. Not wanting to tempt fate by stretching time out to pack, I made sure my bags were ready last night. The twins, disregarding every travel tip I've ever given them, throw clothing around the room and stuff suitcases and overnight bags like they're leaving on a world tour.

"What are you *doing*?" I ask, pulling a ski jacket out of Terra's carry-on bag. "Ryan said it's still warm there." She tries to grab it back, but I throw it over her head to Mia. "Just pack some tank tops, hoodies, shorts, and a pair of jeans. And don't bother bringing any product, other than ponytail holders. Humidity hates your hair."

Mia stops packing long enough to dump the contents of another bag onto her bed. Leave-in conditioner, hairspray, a blow-dryer, two different-sized straightening irons, and three brushes lie in a pile, their trip ended before it's even begun. Terra tosses her a handful of hair ties and they both finish packing, leaving the room looking like it was ransacked by aggressively clumsy burglars.

While the Chaos Sisters try to cram the last bit of clothing into their hopelessly overstuffed suitcases, I decide to take one last tour around the house before we leave.

Although we've only lived in this house a few months, I've fallen in love with it. Mama spends her days keeping every inch gleaming with lemon-scented polish, and we finally got her used to buying fresh flowers instead of plastic. Every Wednesday she takes her cart to the farmers' market downtown and fills it with local food and fresh flowers.

With Eva missing in action, the house is usually quiet, except for Mama's music in the afternoons. When the house is empty, I sit alone in the living room—breathing the scent of lemon and fresh-cut roses, the sound of the breakers below whispering distant secrets—and feel the house wrap itself around me. Sunlight makes the stained-glass windows sparkle like antique jewels. I feel like I'm in an old movie and at any moment a young man in a suit and fedora, holding a bouquet in one hand, might burst through the front door looking for his young bride. This house is drunk with romance.

I take one last peek into the library. Its tomes and their secrets will have to wait until I get back from New Orleans. They've been here for years, since before I was even born; a few more weeks won't hurt. Knowing I can return to the security of these book-lined shelves and the comfort of my brick fireplace makes it easier to face a city I've never been to, to find a woman I thought I knew—my mother, who was never a mother.

Between me and the twins, our list of questions goes on for miles. The most important one: *How could you? How could you leave your children, only to return and masquerade as our aunt?*

We've heard Mama's abbreviated side of the story: Eva left when the twins were two and I was one, and she stepped in to raise us. When pressed as to why she let us believe she was our mother, she only says, "It was for the best." Mia feels this is the single least acceptable answer possible and hasn't spoken more than a couple of words to Mama since.

Once we've loaded our bags and suitcases in the back of Cheddar's pickup truck, it's time to say our goodbyes. Under gray clouds, Mama stands on one side of the walkway and we on the other. "Please call me when you find her." I sense Mama can't bring herself to say Eva's name; she's close enough to tears as it is.

Mia doesn't look up from her own sandals. I can see her jaw clenching, but to her credit, she says nothing. I stay where I am and assure Mama we'll call, while Terra crosses the divide and hugs her tight, swaying just a bit. I know she's calming Mama without saying a word, opening her heart and pouring all the love she has into a woman who only did what she thought was right; who raised us alone while keeping her own daughter's secrets locked painfully away.

Mama strokes the back of Terra's hair, then straightens up and takes her by the shoulders. "You've got to get going. Be safe." Without another word, just a parting glance at each of us, she turns and goes back inside.

"Alright, ladies, let's do this," Cheddar says as he opens the passenger door.

Mia immediately jumps in front, pulling her seat forward just enough to let Terra and me cram ourselves into a back compartment about one size up from a shoebox. "So," I mutter into Mia's ear over the back of her seat, "when we're on The Hill and I throw up, you don't mind that it's going down the back of your shirt?"

We call Highway 17 The Hill. It's the main road between Santa Cruz and San Jose, and it's as treacherous as it is scenic—especially in the rain. Even the most experienced drivers can't know what lies around the next curve. When the steep hills are wet—or, worse, iced over—it can be almost impossible to stop as quickly as you sometimes need to. On any given day the highway is strewn with pieces of cars that never reached their destinations.

Every time we take The Hill, Mia stares out the window at all the people who've died while driving it. They stand just beyond the trees, waiting, in case anyone else meets the same fate. Mia says when a person dies suddenly, they may not even realize they're dead. So they don't get lost in the woods, a guide will show them the way. She says they're gray and slender, almost blending in with the mist and trees—silent sentinels who hope never to be called into action, but too often are.

Sometimes I've envied Mia's ability to see through the multiverse and interact with people on different planes of reality, including people long dead. Driving along The Hill is not one of those times.

Just before my coffee makes its way back up my throat, we reach the summit, where the fog dissipates and we ride into warm, golden sunlight. Early fall can be hotter than most summer days, and suddenly the truck feels oppressively stuffy. Cheddar rolls down the windows as we reach the straightaway. It's a smooth ride the rest of the way to the airport and, thanks to Mia, for the first time in his entire life, Cheddar can afford to leave his wheels in long-term parking. After we've parked and he's checked the truck from every angle to make sure it's clear of any other car that might dent it, we make our way through the bustling airport.

Going through security with the twins is a feat. All our shoes, belts, jewelry, bags and purses piled into the bins look like a holiday sale at the mall. A security officer lifts an eyebrow as our stuff comes out the other side of the x-ray machine, three bins per girl. Cheddar didn't even need one; he just put his phone, keys, and wallet into his shoes and shoved them through, easy-peasy. Once we've reassembled ourselves, we head to the gate, where he's waited for at least five minutes.

Terra can tell he's nervous, so she tells him to sit next to her while we wait to board. Her talent for manipulating the molecular vibrations of the world around her relaxes Cheddar in no time, without his ever catching on; using her own heartbeat as a baseline, she's woven an invisible field of vibration around him that lulls him into a state of pure contentment. She smiles at us, then Cheddar does too—a big, loopy grin. All shall be well in his world for the duration of the flight.

Aboard the plane, I buckle in beside Mia. "So, girlie, any idea how you're going to handle the reunion with our mother?"

"Sure, Em," she snarks. "I'm going to say, 'Congratulations, you've given birth to three healthy girls. Oh, wait—that was a decade and a half ago!'"

"Humor as a weapon," I say, opening a bag of Swedish Fish I brought on board. "I like it."

"And how are *you* going to handle the reunion with Ryan?"

"Hadn't thought about it much." I say it much too quickly to be convincing, and the first of my gummy fishes falls out of my mouth, losing itself between the seat cushions.

In all honesty, I've thought about it a lot, but I'm still not clear on how I feel. It's been long enough that I've gotten used to Ryan being far away, but not so long that I've forgotten how I felt around him—like coming home after being gone for too long, the very opposite of homesickness. It was electric, sweet, and comforting. It was also strange, like I was in a dream that couldn't possibly hold up to scrutiny by the light of day. I prefer being the architect of my own life, and the variable of a boyfriend doesn't fit into that blueprint. At least, not yet.

Waiting for takeoff, I see the sadness in Mia's reflected face as she looks out the window. I wonder if *she* sees it. As angry as she is at Eva, I know she's just barely holding her pain beneath the surface, trying not to let it break free and swallow her whole. We went so long without knowing our mother had left us—and getting along just fine, mind you—part of me wishes Aracelia hadn't told us. But I suppose the truth had to come out eventually. In another year, I tell myself—or five, or ten—it might have hurt worse. It would have been that many more years of deception, and of Mama keeping herself sick with the weight of her secret.

I try to remember if there were clues we missed.

Clues we might have chosen to miss. Did Mama ever say anything strange about Eva, or vice versa—something that didn't add up? Did they ever exchange a telling look in front of us? Were there any inconsistencies in the anecdotes we heard a hundred times growing up? I can't remember. But I'll go over it in my mind for the rest of my life.

For now, I have to find a way to live with it. Live around it, make peace with it, and not let it drag me to the dark place where Mia's found herself. Terra's handling it the best of all; she feels everyone else's pain so close to her own heart, her empathy protects her from anger. I don't know if her charm is a blessing or a curse, but she's keeping herself so busy soothing the rest of us, I'll go with blessing.

Cheddar chats quietly with her, blissfully unaware that she's holding him carefully in her vibratory waves. She looks at me with a huge smile and shrugs. I wink at her, then lay my head back and close my eyes. The best way to speed up the time spent in flight is to just sleep through it. A six-hour flight can feel like an hour if you just let the low hum of the plane lull you to sleep.

I drift off and begin to dream. I'm underwater again, but this time I'm alone. Soft light filters down through the waves and sparkles like gold. I'm slowly treading water beneath the surface, with my hair swirling around my head. Watery sunlight reaches me from above. I want to swim up to it, but I feel so heavy I can only stay where I am. The current gently pushes me back and forth and I feel like I'll fall asleep again, under the water.

Someone grabs my hand, startling me. I can't see their face, but the grip is strong. I'm pulled with urgency through the jade-colored kelp, illuminated by pale light. I don't feel afraid but suddenly I'm being yanked, over and over. I pull back my hand as hard as I can, forcing myself awake.

Mia's pulling on my hand. "We're landing soon. What were you dreaming about? You were mumbling in your sleep."

"Really? Awesome. That doesn't make me want to die of embarrassment at all."

"Better than drooling," says Mia, nodding across the aisle. I turn and see Cheddar, sleeping deeply with his face smashed against the window. He's snoring and his mouth is wide open; as reported, drool is threatening to make its exit from the side of it. Terra pulls a handful of napkins from her purse and stuffs a few in his mouth. He opens his eyes and stares ahead for a moment, no doubt trying to figure out where, exactly, he is. He turns to look at Mia and me and smiles a big, napkin-filled smile.

After what seems like a thousand people get off the plane before us, we take our turn to grab our carry-on bags and thank the pilot on our way out. Cheddar helps us gather our suitcases at baggage claim. I feel sorry for him—you can't even see his face with all he's carrying. He doesn't mind, of course. Cheddar's the kind of friend who would push a piano up a mountain for you and claim he did it for the fresh air.

When we walk outside, the air feels like velvet on

my skin. It's warm and gentle and wraps its arms around me. Walking behind my sisters, I'm mesmerized by their thick black hair fluttering and billowing in the strong breeze, momentarily forgetting we're supposed to be looking for Ryan.

The girls find a place to wait and Cheddar sets down our luggage. "This is nice," he says cheerfully, looking around. "So tropical."

I set my bags down. "You like this? You'd love Hawaii. Same air, better beaches."

"Don't sell this place short. I've read up on the area. It's supposed to be MAGICAL," he replies, like he's trying to sell a vacation timeshare.

"Oh, I'll give it a fair chance. I just mean you'd love Hawaii. We should take you sometime."

His eyes light up. "Yes. Yes, you should."

I'm sure Mia will want to bring him on our next trip. More to the point, I doubt Mama would let us take a trip anywhere without him. Now that we're older, she trusts the world less and Cheddar all the more. He's our guardian, our protector, and as far as Mama is concerned, he's family.

As he sits down next to Mia and Terra, I walk to the curb to watch for Ryan. He didn't say what kind of car he'd be driving and all I can see is a long line of taxis. People are queued up along a velvet rope waiting for rides into town. I cross my arms and crane my neck, scanning the local foot traffic. No one looks familiar.

As I turn to rejoin Cheddar and the girls, I stop dead in my tracks. Ryan's walking toward us. He's smiling.

His hair is cropped short and he's got on his usual white T-shirt, jeans, and black mechanic boots. The ever-present chain from his wallet to his belt loop gleams in the Southern sun. I'd love to say the sight of him makes my heart jump—that I could just run over and hug him.

But next to him, also coming our way, is Colin.

CHAPTER
2

BEFORE I CAN REACT, Ryan and Colin reach our group. Mia and Terra stand wide-eyed and speechless, until Cheddar protectively steps in front of us. "Are you kidding me?" Mia groans, pushing him out of the way. She faces the Laurent brothers, glaring side to side at both of them.

"Hey, Mia," Ryan says as he moves past her to hug me. I'm still not able to speak, and the words in my head don't seem appropriate for polite conversation anyway.

"What's *he* doing here?" Mia demands.

Colin stands perfectly still, arms crossed. He studies Mia's face and petite frame. As small as she is, she's also formidable. At first I think he's sizing up the enemy, but then a flicker of what looks like admiration crosses his face. Mia, per usual, is having none of it.

"Relax; Colin wants to help," Ryan tells her, breaking our hug. He goes to shake Cheddar's hand. "Good to see you, man."

Cheddar takes his eyes off Colin long enough to look at his twin brother. "Yeah, you too." He looks from one to the other. I can tell he's mentally cataloging their subtle differences in appearance.

Ryan looks rested and put together—shirt spotless; face clean-shaven. In contrast, Colin looks exhausted. While short on the sides and back, his hair is longer than Ryan's, falling over sunken eyes. A light beard shadows his jaw. He could be handsome, but looks like he hasn't slept in days.

"He's a freak," Mia growls, disregarding Colin's presence. "We don't need his help." This evokes a low laugh from Colin, which throws her into a rage. "Who do you think you are? You stalk our family, threaten my sister, and now you're *laughing* at me?" She's advanced to within a couple feet of Colin by the time Cheddar and Terra manage to pull her back. Mia's eyes flash with anger. She's so upset she doesn't notice Terra working to calm her down. The twins sit together while Terra weaves a tranquil vibration around us all.

"Why does he want to help us?" I finally ask Ryan, loud enough for everyone to hear.

Before he can answer, Colin speaks up. "A friend of mine is missing. I need to find him just as much as you need to find that book. Your aunt caused a lot of trouble and hurt a lot of people here in New Orleans when she took it. But as much as I want to blame the Tempest family for everything that's gone wrong, it won't help me find my friend."

Mia recovers enough to answer Colin without lunging for his throat. "Amazingly, we agree on how much trouble she's caused. But she's not our aunt. In fact, as far as I'm concerned, she isn't anything."

Ryan looks at me, shaking his head. He hasn't told Colin, who stares at Mia. "What do you mean?"

Gently stroking Mia's hair, Terra answers softly, "She's our birth mother."

Colin is clearly thrown for a second, but never takes his eyes off Mia. It's starting to get a little weird.

"Can we go now?" I ask Ryan.

We can sort out just how helpful Colin intends to be later. Right now, I need food and a shower.

Ryan has a van in short-term parking for us and, surprisingly, Colin offers to help Cheddar carry the luggage. He tries to pick up one of Mia's bags but she rips it out of his hands as we load the dingy yellow van, whose many rust spots, dents, and scratches have been plastered over with New Orleans Saints stickers. Thankfully, Terra keeps the good vibe going as we pile in; because Cheddar's the easiest mark, he's in a great mood and takes the front passenger seat next to Colin.

The irony that Colin's behind the wheel isn't lost on me. With the twins in the middle seat and Ryan and me in the back, I have a clear view of everyone and everything. There is no way I'm turning my back on Colin.

"*Frère*, drive to the Quarter so we can get some food in the French Market," Ryan says as he leans back and puts his arm behind me. It's not so much that he's trying to get his arm around my shoulders—he's not even touching me; he just leans it on the back of the seat. All the same, feeling him so close makes my cheeks flush with heat.

Driving through the neighborhoods on our way to the French Quarter, we can see the scars of Hurricane Katrina still starkly visible. So much of the city still hasn't been restored, and it's clear the storm took more than property and vehicles when it swept through. It took lives, both human and animal. It took entire communities, breaking thousands of hearts as the water dragged hopes and futures down to where they couldn't be recovered. Empty storefronts and boarded homes stand in silent rows like desolate tombstones.

And yet, as we near the Quarter, the heart of the city beats louder. Second-floor balconies held up by intricate wrought-iron railings overflow with lush green ferns and Mardi Gras beads. Halloween decorations and sugar skulls appear around every corner as people shop and walk their dogs. Street-level doors are flanked by brightly painted shutters—red, yellow, aquamarine. Tourists and locals intermingle while street musicians fill the alleys with jazz and blues.

As we get closer to the open-air market and the food that my stomach now demands, Ryan points out the gas-burning lamps that adorn the buildings and brick alleyways. "They burn all day and night, always."

"Why?"

"Ambiance mainly," he says, rubbing his chin. "They don't throw a whole lot of light when it's dark out. Nothing like the neon lights on Bourbon Street."

We find a place to park and walk a few blocks to the market. Ryan and Cheddar talk while Colin walks a few steps ahead. The twins and I hang back to have a chat of our own.

"The vibration here is amazing!" Terra whispers. She's right; even without possessing her particular charm, Mia and I can feel it too. Hundreds of years of history seem to bubble up around us with every step we take.

Mia's seeing an entirely different cityscape. "So many people," she whispers. "Native Americans, French, Haitians. Pirates, too—and they really like *you*, Emerald." Turning to look at someone we can't see, she shouts, "Hey, fancy-pants—*beat it!*"

Ryan stops walking and looks back. Seeing no one but us, he arches an eyebrow at me. I answer with a shake of the head: *Don't ask.*

As we enter the market, we're immersed in New Orleans culture. There's a different band playing on every block and loud laughter mixes with the music. The smell of food cooking makes my stomach growl, and kiosk after kiosk is laden with local artworks and crafts—paintings in festive reds and soulful blues, sculpture, handmade musical instruments, and jewelry that glitters in the sun. Men seated at a makeshift counter laugh and yell while eating oysters as fast as the guy behind the counter can shuck them.

The boys go to order food from a woman with a colorful scarf piled high on her head. Cheddar returns with a huge smile and eyes wide. "Here," he says, "try these." In his hand is a red-and-white paper tray overflowing with batter-fried nuggets and lemon wedges.

"What is it?" Terra asks as she reaches for one.

"Gator bites!" Cheddar says as though he's just unlocked the secret to life.

Terra's hand pulls back faster than my eye can follow. "Pass, thanks."

Colin leans in and takes one, offering it to Mia. "They're really good."

Not one to back down from a challenge, Mia snatches it and takes a bite. We all watch as she chews. She tilts her head, like she's listening to something, and slowly nods. "Not bad. Like a mix of chicken and fish. Pretty tender."

"I'm not eating lizard." Terra shudders.

Ryan joins us holding two trays of fried green tomatoes. "You haven't lived until you've tasted these," he announces proudly.

"That's more my speed," Terra says as she takes a tray.

I take one from her and try not to swallow it whole. The fried breading is crisp and perfectly seasoned. The warm green tomato melts in my mouth. I close my eyes and savor it. I want fifteen more, immediately.

After Cheddar finishes his second po'-boy sandwich, overflowing with fried shrimp, lettuce and tomato, we head to Café du Monde to try the beignets. I'm still hungry, and as the cashier hands me the warm bag, I peer in and see three pieces of deep-fried dough, swimming in what appears to be two cups of powdered sugar. We find a seat outdoors under an expansive green-and-white striped awning. Terra's throwing pieces of beignet into Cheddar's mouth. Without fail, he catches every one. It's almost superhuman.

Across the street is a large square filled with artists, fortunetellers, and tourists. A church towers over the far side. "That's Jackson Square and St. Louis Cathedral," Ryan tells us. "It's the oldest Catholic church in the country."

A brass band begins to play, filling the square with music. Several couples spontaneously start dancing.

"Come on," Ryan says. He pulls me up before I can protest. With my hand in his, we run across the street and into the square. He spins me around to face him and I start doing something that can't possibly be described as dancing. As clumsy as I feel, the music is infectious. The drum and tuba provide a beat that I'm unable to resist. Ryan laughs as he moves his shoulders back and forth, his smile dissolving the last of my reservations.

I understand the magic of this place. Music floats on the breeze like the scent of magnolia, drawing you to it, making your heart race. There's a constant flow of people, from around the corner and around the world, making it feel exotic and like home at the same time.

The music slows and instead of letting me go, Ryan pulls me closer, swaying us both back and forth. Resting my head on his shoulder, I see an elderly couple nearby, holding each other tight as though they were one person. The woman smiles at me and I wonder to myself how many times they've danced in this same square.

Not wanting the moment to end, I take a deep breath, and as I exhale, time slows. Everything around us seems to dissolve and the music recedes into the distance. I can feel Ryan's heart beating in real time, steady and true.

His pulse is unaffected by the slowing of time. He smells like Dial soap and cinnamon toothpaste, and I take in another deep breath so I'll never forget the way the scents mix together.

He pulls back and looks into my eyes, his own brown eyes catching the glow of the late-afternoon light. He brings his face closer to mine, and although I think he's going to kiss me, he only brushes his cheek against mine. "I'm glad you're here," he murmurs. "There's so much I want to show you."

As soon as the words leave his lips, it starts to sprinkle. The band moves under the portico of the church, but as the artists and fortunetellers cover their tables, people carry on dancing. The rain is warm and gentle. This city has seen far worse without letting the party die.

I let time resume its normal pace as we look up and let the rain hit our faces. The drops are making small dots on Ryan's shirt. He takes my hand and leads me back to the café. As we cross the street, he keeps hold of my hand, gently rubbing his thumb over mine. It comforts me and I don't pull away from it, even though I'm sure I'll hear about it later from the twins.

"Nothing like dancing in the square as a welcome to the Quarter," Ryan says.

Terra's smiling at me. Mia, not so much.

Colin is nowhere to be seen. I look around, then to Cheddar, who's sprawled belly up on the nearest park bench and has clearly helped himself to the rest of the beignets. He's got powdered sugar all over his shirt and looks a little comatose. "Colin went to get the van," he manages to say, reading the concern on my face. "He's in a hurry to get us to wherever we're staying. Works for me…I could use a nap."

"A nap and about six thousand sit-ups," Mia quips.

"How far is this place we're staying?" I ask Ryan. His cousin runs the Laurent family's old plantation well outside the French Quarter, which they partially converted into a local history museum. The place is well known and secure, which was enough information to satisfy Mama.

Ryan smiles. "It's in Vacherie—another forty-five minutes, give or take. Not many tourists out that way, and it's home to a lot of good people. You'll love it."

Colin rolls the van up to the curb; the girls help a groaning Cheddar up from the bench.

The ride to Vacherie takes us west, past lush green fields and rows of live oak, myrtle, and magnolia trees. Spanish moss hangs like ragged gauze from the oak branches. The sprinkle has turned to a proper downpour, and watching the scenery go by is like peering into a clouded looking-glass. The sun, muted by dark clouds, covers the landscape in an ominous glow.

With the exception of the hum from the engine, the van is quiet. Cheddar's asleep, and the rearview mirror permits me to see Colin stealing glances at Mia. She stares out her window, oblivious, but I see it and I don't like it. The odd thing is that when he looks at her, his face softens. For the first time since I've known him, there's no anger or pain visible—like looking at her allows him to relax and put his guard down.

I still don't like it.

After an hour on the road, we pull into a wide, circular driveway and stop in front of a large and cheerful yellow house. An expansive covered porch with two separate sets of stairs offers shelter from the rain.

As we gather at the front door, bags in hand, Ryan pulls me aside. "Take the night to settle in and rest," he whispers. "Tomorrow, after breakfast, we'll come back to get you. We have a lot of ground to cover to find your aunt…" He trails off, looking down at the porch floor. "Sorry—your mom."

"It's okay," I say, smiling up at him. "We're not used to saying it either."

A woman in her mid-twenties—wearing a black raincoat, boots, and stylishly tattered jeans—opens the door and, on first sight of Ryan, breaks into a beaming smile. Looking right past Colin without a word, she surveys the rest of us, her twinkling eyes alighting on me. "Welcome to Laurent Plantation. You must be Emerald. The other two look like a matched set of salt and pepper shakers."

The girls look at each other, unsure how to take it.

To my surprise, the woman hugs me. "I'm glad you've come. We're going to excuse Ryan and his brother for the evening and get you girls and your strapping friend here settled in. What is your name, sir?"

"Chet, but everyone calls me Cheddar." He's visibly bashful to introduce himself in a shirt that's covered in powdered sugar, but offers his hand just the same.

"Like the cheese? All right, then," she chuckles,

shaking his hand. "I'm Rosamie Laurent, but you can call me Rose."

"Like the flower?" Cheddar grins, proud of himself.

"Nothing much gets past you, now, does it?" she says, returning the smile.

After dismissing Ryan and Colin for the evening, Rose gives us a tour of the house and grounds. The furniture and family heirlooms are simple but spotless, and sugar-cookie candles burn throughout the house. Outside, rainwater fills an arrangement of huge metal bowls to the brim.

"Those funny-looking cisterns used to be for boiling cane juice down to sugar," Rose tells us. "They're called coppers, but they're really made from iron. Now we just use them to catch rain and host frogs." She smiles. "We've been on this land since 1805. The women in our family called the shots then, and we still do today. If you need anything, check with me first. You have any problems, I'll handle them."

I have no doubt in my mind that she will.

She leads us to a set of guest houses at the rear of the property. Each is painted the same bright yellow as the main house, with small covered porches surrounded by thick palms. A black cat with pale-green eyes sits in a rocking chair, seemingly waiting to greet us.

"That's Miracle. If you like cats, she'll keep you company. If you don't, she'll keep you company anyway." Rose opens the door and ushers me and the girls inside, stopping Cheddar at the threshold. "You're next door, boss. I'll check on you in a minute." She dismisses him and he does as he's told. "Now, if you girls get cold at night, which you will, start yourself a fire," she says, pointing to a small brick fireplace. Seeing it makes me homesick for Mr. McHenry's library. "There are feather beds for you to sleep on, and extra blankets if you need them. If the power goes out, which it will, you have plenty of candles and a lantern. If you get scared, which you shouldn't, come on up to the main house. I don't sleep much and when I do, I've one ear always listening. I'm available any time you need me, and you have Miracle to keep watch with those big green eyes of hers."

Before going to check on Cheddar, Rose invites us to dinner and steps out, closing the door behind her.

"I like her," Terra says. "Her vibration is steady and grounded."

"What do you think, Mia?" I ask as we unpack.

"She's great, minus the 'salt and pepper shakers' crack," Mia sighs, but her snark is only at about half power. Something else is bothering her. "This place is crawling with people," she says, looking all around. "I'll be lucky to get any sleep. They're all talking about someone called Madame DéSolé. They keep saying she's waiting for us… we'd better be careful."

"That didn't take long," I say, suddenly feeling very tired. "We haven't been here one full day and we're already in trouble."

"It's exciting," Terra enthuses. "And we've got Miracle here to keep us company. She's charmed too, somehow— like she's got bees buzzing all around her. I wonder how they do that?" she muses as Miracle walks a figure-eight pattern between and around her legs, brushing against her from all sides.

"I'm not sure I want to know," I say as I pull aside the curtains and gaze into the gathering dark. The main house is lit up and I can see Rosamie in the kitchen laughing with Cheddar. He's either hungry again, or a bit charmed himself.

"What's the plan for tomorrow?" asks Mia.

"After breakfast, Ryan and Colin will pick us up." Outside, the garden palms sway gently in the evening breeze. "We should try to find Eva as soon as possible," I say, turning away from the window.

Mia doesn't look up from unpacking her suitcase. I know she doesn't want to see Eva. I can't imagine how the conversation will go once we find her, but we have to get that book back.

"We'll find her," assures Terra, opting to use words rather than her special power to calm me. "It's what we came to do, and we will. But it's late. Worrying won't do anything but deprive us of our beauty sleep, and Mia *really needs it*."

It's not as mean as it sounds; I've never seen Mia scowling so hard. Her gape of mock horror at Terra's wisecrack is pretty funny, though. They laugh and tease each other mercilessly, until it comes out that Terra knows for certain what I only suspected based on the look I glimpsed in the rearview: "Colin likes Mia!"

Mia's response is to make a third, harder-to-identify face; a face someone might make if she found out she's having mud for dinner. "What? No way."

"Oh, yes way," Terra insists. "As soon as he saw you at the airport, I felt it. His vibrations sort of…got more intense in a way, but calmer in another way; more harmonized."

Mia shakes her head. "You're the one who needs sleep, sister. You're babbling."

"He kept looking at you when we were in the van," I dutifully put in, turning back to the window. I swear the darkness has deepened, the shadows grown more inky black, in just the few moments I looked away.

"Ugh." Mia flings herself back into the feather pillows behind her. "You get the nice one, and I get the creeper? No. No. No."

"I don't think he's a creeper," Terra says. "He's just had a hard life. You know—like Eva."

Good as Terra's intentions are, her words don't exactly put Colin on Mia's good side. That's the thing about words: compared to our charms, they're a little hit-or-miss. I feel bad for Terra. She tried.

No one says anything for a few moments. Without the aid of my own special power, they feel like hours, but I've found it's not always wise to fast-forward through life's awkward bits just because I can. Terra strokes Miracle's sleek, black fur. "People can change," she says at last, in a small, hopeful voice.

After changing into dry clothes, we make our way along a brick path toward the main house. The rain has stopped for now, and the light from my lantern casts shadows that dance in the mist rising from the palms. Frogs croak and sing as the dark fully settles around us.

Halfway to the house, something catches Mia's eye and she stops us.

"What is—"

Cutting me off with a "*Shh*," Mia takes the lantern from me and holds it above our heads, squinting into the darkness.

"Here we go again," Terra whispers. Mia's field of vision is always crowded with people the rest of us can't see, so her stopping to check on them comes as no surprise.

Mia raises the lantern higher above her head and fixes her gaze on a point somewhere beyond the palms. Miracle has followed us and now sits at Mia's feet, peering in the same direction. She sits completely still, except the tip of her tail, which flicks from side to side in anticipation.

"Hey, cat lady, what do you see?" I ask, getting a little twitchy myself.

Mia doesn't take her eyes from the expanse of darkness beneath the palms. "There are people out in the field, just past the property line. They're watching us."

"So? You said there were people *everywhere* here."

"I know." Mia's lantern hand trembles, causing the handle to squeak a little, and the shadows of the tall grasses to shudder. "But these people aren't dead."

CHAPTER
3

THE DARKNESS AND MIST make it impossible to see our watchers clearly. Ghostly white clothing is the only thing that stands out; their faces, featureless masks in the night. Mia douses the lantern so we can blend into the shadows, leveling the playing field.

"Their vibrations feel strange," Terra whispers. "Like they can't think for themselves...."

The figures begin to move, causing the three of us to try to hide ourselves in the shadows. But they aren't advancing; the dark made it impossible to tell until they were noticeably smaller, but they're actually receding from view.

Just as the night swallows our prowlers completely, the rain returns.

We hurry into the warmth and light of the main house to find Cheddar draining a huge pot of boiled crawfish over the kitchen sink. The average guy his age couldn't lift half its weight, and I see him glance over his shoulder to make sure Rosamie notices.

"Eyes on your work, hot stuff," blurts Mia as we speed-walk through the kitchen; "steam burns are serious business." She's white as a sheet from the scare we got outside, but unable to help herself. Sass is like breathing for her—maybe an even higher priority, considering I don't think any of us has taken a breath since bolting out of the yard.

In any case, Cheddar's face flushes as red as the crawfish by the time we hit the other end of the kitchen. Admittedly, it's a *very* big kitchen.

Blues music fills the vast dining room, and what seems like hundreds of candles are lit in case the power goes out. We seat ourselves at an expansive table set with vintage dishes and crystal glassware that reflect the candles' twinkling light. Curls of steam rise from fresh-baked French bread, and a platter of fried green tomatoes sits right across from me. I nudge it a bit closer to my plate in a shameless bid for the first helping. As Rose pours iced tea, Cheddar places a ceramic platter of crawfish and potatoes in the middle of the table. The smell of garlic and bay leaves mingling with the scent of the bread is almost more than I can bear.

Before we eat, Rose offers a blessing. "May our paths be clear of threat, our hearts full of peace, and all our good prayers answered. Now, eat!"

After we've consumed far more calories in one sitting than most physicians would probably advise for an entire day, we all pitch in to clean the kitchen before gathering in the living room in front of a crackling fire. Cheddar falls asleep in his chair almost immediately.

Rose turns to me and the girls. "After a good night's sleep, I suppose you'll start the search for your mother?"

The question takes me off guard for a moment, but it's not a total surprise that Ryan has told her a little about what brought us here. "Yes," I begin carefully, "we… need to find her as soon as possible. She took something that's got to be returned to its rightful owners."

"You're looking for the book," Rose guesses.

"That and a few answers," says Mia, staring into the fire.

Rose studies her for a moment. "You want to know why she left you to be raised by your grandmother."

I guess Ryan went ahead and told her *everything*. "What do you know about the book?" I ask in a valiant attempt to steer the conversation away from Eva.

Rose looks at me and smiles, honoring my effort. With a theatrical flourish of her hand she says, "That old book has bounced around for as long as I can remember. Family lore will tell you it contains secrets to transporting oneself to different times and places; that it holds conjures which give its reader unlimited powers."

At this point she has our full attention, except Cheddar, who's likely dreaming of the pecan pie that awaits us in the kitchen.

"Oh, don't look so spooked," Rose chuckles, reading the apprehension in our faces. "It's all a bunch of nonsense. There is no power in that book that the three of you don't already hold."

In an instant, apprehension becomes alarm, and of course this doesn't get by her either.

"Yes, I know all about your family," she says, winking. "About your charms."

"How?" asks Terra.

"Stories get told and retold around here," Rose tells her with an enigmatic smile. "As wild as they may sound, plenty have a backbone of truth to them. As for the book, what it does contain may be of value after all, but that's up to you to find out for yourselves. Just remember that not everything is entirely what it seems, and know that you aren't the only ones desperate to find that book."

"Believe us, we know," Mia interjects. "Colin wants it."

"Indeed, he does. But he wants it for all the wrong reasons. That dusty old thing holds no answers for him—only the promise of power. The person you must watch out for is DéSolé Marchand."

"Madame DéSolé?" asks Terra.

"You've heard of her!" Rose laughs. "She loves to throw that Madame around; tries to make herself sound imposing. The only power that old girl has is the power of persuasion. She's picked up some tricks here and there from the Cajun women, but there's nothing Voodoo about her."

Mia looks unconvinced. I'm sure she's thinking about the people who watched us from beyond the trees.

Rose leans forward and looks us earnestly in the eyes. "Listen—you girls were gifted your charms. You were born with them, and I'm sure by now you're learning that they're most powerful when combined. This might make Ms. Marchand a bit jealous, but she'll never be as strong as the three of you together. You'll do well to keep that in mind."

Cheddar stirs a bit and Rose looks over. "Where y' at, big boy? There's pie in the kitchen with your name on a nice, big slice of it. Do us a blessing and go cut some up."

"Don't have to ask me twice," he says before stretching and peeling himself out of the chair he's melted into.

Rose watches him go, then turns back to us and continues in a hushed tone. "What you must know is that Colin wants that book more than anybody else does. He thinks it holds the key to finding his friend, Wyatt. That boy went missing in the swamp. There's talk that Wyatt met his end at Colin's hands."

Mia shifts in her seat; Terra sets a comforting hand on her knee.

"If I had to testify," Rose continues, "I couldn't say I know whether he did or didn't, but I *will* say that as long as I've known Colin, he's been ready to do whatever it takes to get what he wants. Mind him and his actions; he doesn't have the soft heart that Ryan does." She looks at me and smiles. "We've heard plenty about you, Emerald. Ryan could hardly talk about anything else when he got back from Santa Cruz. I can see you took a shine to him too, though you strike me as a girl who isn't easily knocked off her center."

"No, ma'am," I say truthfully. "I'm not."

"Well, that's good! Women here are strong, and there's always room for more like you. Now, how about some pie? Need to get at it before it ends up nothing more than crumbs in the tin."

She's got Cheddar's number. The only thing that isn't safe around our friend-slash-bodyguard is food.

After we've demolished the pie and said our goodnights, we step outside to a clear sky and full moon. Every leaf on every plant seems to glow in the moonlight.

Miracle, an attentive hostess, awaits us with flicking tail. The coast must be clear, as she turns and patters down the walkway without a care, letting us know, with frequent glances back, that we are to follow her home right away.

We tuck ourselves into bed, and our feline chaperone curls up at Mia's feet.

"Terra," I say, fighting eyelids that are heavy with exhaustion, "I need you to try and get a read on Colin tomorrow."

"Mmm, okay," is all she says, all anyone says, for the rest of the night. The day's travel, its revelations, and the staggering amount of food we've managed to eat has caught up with us, and I sink into a deep, dreamless sleep.

#

We wake the next morning to Miracle scratching at the door to go out. Mia strokes her head before opening the heavy wooden door to a gloriously sunny sky. She shields her eyes against the glare as Rosamie greets us.

Bright-eyed and fully dressed, Rose appears to have been up for hours. "Mornin'!" she chirps. "Get yourselves presentable. There's coffee in the kitchen and my cousins will come soon to fetch you."

Cheddar's room is empty; I'm sure whatever breakfast they made has long since met its end.

We dress and head to the main house for coffee to drink on the front porch while watching for Ryan and Colin. Stretching out in front of us, the landscape is lush and green. Spanish moss drips the last of the night's rainwater onto palm leaves, where it sparkles like jewels; the warm, wet air smells sweet and clean.

Rosamie joins us on the porch. Even without makeup, she's beautiful. Her brown eyes sparkle with a light of their own, and her skin glows with a natural, rosy blush. She'd look delicate if not for the sharp jawline, which complements and enhances her beauty with the suggestion of strength.

She points to the oaks in front of the porch. "See the plants creeping up these trees?" Some kind of leafy plant covers the oaks' trunks and the undersides of their thick branches. "That's resurrection fern. It can go for what seems like forever without water. Curls up when it's dry, which isn't often in these parts. It's grown here for over a hundred years. Beautiful and resilient—a good way to be," she says admiringly.

"With the amount of rain we've had in California lately, it would dry up and never uncurl," Mia says, lifting a section of Terra's hair to examine it disapprovingly.

"Check your own split ends!" Terra says indignantly, smacking her hand away.

The twins debate over who's in greater need of a deep conditioning as Ryan and Colin's old van trundles into view. They stop bickering as it lurches to a stop in front of the house and the boys hop out.

Ryan smiles at me and I can't help smiling back.

"Y'all, don't these girls look as pretty as gardenia blooms?" Rose calls out.

Ryan beams. "Yes, ma'am, they do."

Colin rearranges gravel with the toe of his boot, saying nothing.

Cheddar steps out the front door with two large canvas bags. Rosamie runs to him, grabbing them away with a laugh. "Who put you in charge of the lunches I made?" she teases. Handing the bags to me, she adds under her breath, "I'm afraid my po'-boys don't stand much chance of lasting 'til noon."

"I'm powerless against your culinary skills, Rose," Cheddar grins.

Colin, getting impatient, clears his throat.

"Right," says Ryan. "Time to go."

We load ourselves and our lunches into the van. Ryan gets behind the wheel and motions me to the passenger seat. The last to get in is Mia, whose only choice is a seat beside Colin. She hesitates at the door, wrinkling her nose like she just opened a carton of spoiled milk, before sliding in next to him with a sigh.

Not too keen on the arrangement myself, I cock my head to keep an eye on them. Mia's squished as far to her side as she can get, like she wants to squeeze out through the two-inch opening in her window.

After riding for several minutes—quietly calculating the most awkward possible way to break the silence, I suppose—Mia asks Colin point blank, "So what happened to your friend, Wyatt?"

He looks at her for the first time since we left the plantation. "Excuse me?"

"Wyatt. Your *friend*," she bites off, and the word has a sickly sound. "The reason you're here. Ring any bells?"

"That's no concern of yours," he shoots back. "Today we're trying to find Mother of the Year."

Mia lets the dig slide. "The way I hear it, he's missing and you had something to do with it. Care to shed some light on that, or are you going to pretend you don't have your own agenda?"

"Mia!" I say, harsher than I mean to.

"Easy," says Ryan, glancing into the rearview. "We can talk about all that later."

Colin smirks at Mia and puts in his earbuds to drown out any further interrogation.

I can't blame him. Mia's anger has been evident to everyone, but that was an undeserved attack. She surely knows from all the law books she's borrowed from Mr. Seville that what Rose told us was only hearsay. I'm no fan of Colin either, but Mia's accusatory tone isn't helping the situation.

While Cheddar and Terra chat, I decide to ask Ryan for a different part of the story. "What do you know about Madame DéSolé?"

"She's a conjure woman with a lot of devotees," he says, keeping his eyes on the road. "Most people are afraid of her, but there are some who ally with her thinking it'll benefit them." He glances in the mirror at Colin, making sure the earbuds are still in. They are, but Ryan lowers his voice just the same. "Colin spent quite a bit of time with her group before Wyatt Breslin disappeared."

"Do you think he had anything to do with what happened to Wyatt?"

"You mean do I think Colin...*hurt* him?" Our voices are barely audible by now.

I nod.

"What I know for sure," Ryan murmurs, "is that Colin had the book before Eva did. He was messing around with the spells to try and go back in time to save our mother. It's ridiculous; nothing in that book could help him do that. The world doesn't work that way. The book is nothing but useless conjures that only a desperate person would even try."

"What do you think did happen to Wyatt?" I ask, watching through the windows as small houses with vast, green yards flicker by.

"Think he got himself lost out in the swamp," Ryan answers matter-of-factly. "Colin thinks he accidentally sent him to a different dimension." Chagrined, he shakes his head. "My brother's completely lost his grip on reality."

I gaze out the driver's-side window at some children jumping rope along the side of the road while a pair of unimpressed, ancient-looking street dogs supervise. Before the merge with my sisters, when our combined powers made such strange things happen, I'd have agreed with Ryan on the impossibility of interdimensional travel. Now, I'm not so sure.

"I'll tell you this," Ryan continues: "Madame DéSolé

wants that book back just as much as Colin does. We need to find Eva before she does, or you may not get a chance to find any answers."

We check a couple of clubs and a restaurant Eva's known to frequent, but find no sign of her. According to Cheddar it's been too long since breakfast, and he's ready to give his full care and consideration to Rosamie's sandwiches. Meanwhile, Terra's begun looking a little stressed. "You okay, Terra?" I ask, but she says she didn't sleep great and it's catching up with her.

Ryan drives us to a sun-drenched dock along one of the hundreds of entrances to the swamp. "We'll take a couple boats out while we eat so you have something to look at other than Colin," he kids while untying a boat that's clearly only going to fit three people. Colin, untying another three-seater a short way up the dock, shoots him a sneer.

Pulling Terra aside, I ask under my breath, "What's the verdict on Colin?"

Terra shrugs. "He doesn't want to hurt any of us. But I've never been in such a small, enclosed space with him for so long at a time as I have these past couple of days. There's only so much of those dark vibrations I can take."

Cheddar, giddily walking to the boats with the two canvas bags of po'-boys slung over one broad shoulder, happens to catch her last few words and slows to give us a weird look. "Vibrations, huh?"

"Did I say that outloud?" Terra asks.

"Yes you did," Cheddar answers, giving us both an

even weirder look before returning his attention to the more interesting business of lunch.

"Terra," I say, placing my hands lovingly on her shoulders, "volume control."

Terra pats my hands and pulls away. "Relax. Come on, let's float." She stretches the travel kinks out of her back and makes straight for the boat with Ryan in it.

"Not so fast," Mia orders from behind us. We turn to see her standing with arms crossed and an indignant expression. "I'm not sitting with Colin this entire trip."

"You don't have to," I say, glancing up the dock to where Cheddar's seated himself in Colin's boat. I figure he probably wants to keep his massive self as close as possible to our group's least trusted member while we're split up and on his turf. I look at Ryan, settling into the other boat with the bag of sandwiches Cheddar just tossed him. We've had exactly zero alone time. Then again, no matter *which* boat I take, we're not going to have any now, either. "I'll ride with Colin and—"

"No," the girls say in unison.

"Not a chance," Mia says, her look defying me to say something about it. Terra nods her agreement.

"Just because you're two years older—"

Terra cuts me off with a "Nope."

"Fine." I turn my back to them and crouch to pick two blades of old grass, one long and one short. Facing my sisters again, I present my closed fist with the two straws sticking out. They draw.

Mia flicks her nub of a straw away with a sigh, heading toward Colin's boat.

"Aw, c'mon Mia, don't be mad. We'll laugh about this later!" Terra calls hopefully after Mia as she jumps into the boat with Ryan and me.

Colin extends a hand to help Mia into their boat. She brushes past it and sits at the front, leaving Colin and Cheddar to sit side by side. "Have it your way," he says as he sits down, offering her a sandwich and a bottle of water. To Mia's credit, she takes them without ripping his hands off.

Ryan and Colin start the engines and it's clear that, after years of navigating these waterways, they know exactly where they're going. Riding under groves of cypress trees heavy with moss and chattering with wild birds, it's like being in another world. The deeper we go into the swamp, the wilder and more beautiful the banks become. Deep purple irises interweave with pale-lavender hyacinth and white spider lilies, their perfume filling the air.

As pretty as it is, I realize that if I were out here alone, I'd be hopelessly lost. Stealing a glance at Colin in the other boat—dappled light and shadow playing on his face as we pass under arching branches—I think of Wyatt and shudder.

We tie up under a thick cluster of trees to eat lunch. Ryan tears a piece off his bread and throws it in the water. "Look, just over there," he says, pointing to a spot near the bank.

In the shade of a tree, with just the upper half of its face above water, an alligator watches with interest. It snaps at the bread but stays put.

"Don't worry, that's a little one," Ryan says, gently tapping me under the chin when he sees my alarm. "Maybe four feet long. He's not interested in you. In fact, he's more scared of you than you are of him."

"Oh, I seriously doubt that," I say.

"Really. We swim in these waters; have since we were little. They try to get away as fast as they can if you approach." He proves his point by stepping out of the boat onto the muddy bank. The gator dips under the water and disappears with a flick of its tail. Ryan picks a handful of irises and hands them to me, smiling. "Now, if you go stomping around a nest of eggs and mama comes at you, that's a different story." He points further up the bank. Following his finger, I see a larger gator sunning herself quietly on a rock, one eye fixed on Ryan. "Not to worry, mama," he says gently; "we'll leave the way we came."

"No stomping eggs—check," I say. "But, no swimming either."

Even with sweat on his forehead, Ryan looks perfectly comfortable. His tanned face betrays no sign of worry. Here in the middle of the swamp, I understand why. The still waters beneath us seem to dissolve my worries for the time being. Watching Ryan watch the gator, I see the love he has for this place. I can't imagine being anywhere other than right here, right now.

I look over to the other boat and see Cheddar and Colin talking. Mia keeps looking toward the bow of their boat, intent on something we can't see.

"Looks like she's got company," Terra murmurs into my ear.

"I noticed too," I whisper. "The last thing Mia wants is more company."

Terra, facing the other boat, closes her eyes, reading her twin sister's vibration with no effort at all. "Mia's fine," she reports, eyes opening. "The attitude is mostly for show at this point. Besides, it's good for Colin. He's way too serious."

"I would be, too, if everyone thought I'd killed my best friend."

After we finish eating, and the alligator finishes the rest of Ryan's sandwich, he shouts to Colin, "You ready to go?"

"Yep," Colin calls back. "It's not going to do anything but get hotter and more humid out here today, and I'd say Mia looks uncomfortable enough already."

"Hm?" Mia pulls her gaze away from the front of their boat long enough to shoot him a distracted glance. "Oh, yeah…humidity."

Ryan tells us it's hotter than usual for the end of October, but he's sure another storm will roll in soon and cool everything down. With Halloween two days away, I hope the rain doesn't spoil our plans to celebrate in the French Quarter.

Back at the dock, Ryan helps Terra and me out of the boat. "I'm sorry we didn't have any luck today," he says, hugging me. "I want to get you back to Rosamie's before dark, but we'll try again tomorrow. I'm sure we'll find her."

Mia hangs back as the boys pile into the van. She's unsettled, which confirms something strange happened during lunch. "What, or who, were you looking at when we were out there?" I ask.

"Yeah," adds Terra, "you feel all jittery."

Mia waits for the van's engine to start before answering: "We have a complication."

I roll my eyes. "When don't we? So who was it?"

"It was Wyatt Breslin."

CHAPTER
4

DESPITE THE HEAT of the afternoon sun, goosebumps cover my arms. Mia seeing Wyatt when no one else can confirms that he's dead.

I suddenly feel like I don't belong here with Ryan and Colin. I just want to be home, in the library, surrounded by the safety and refuge of its books. I don't want to have to tell Ryan that Wyatt is dead, or try to explain how I know this. Colin seems more like the enemy than he ever has, and my legs feel unsteady beneath me.

Mia doesn't seem as concerned as she should be. Terra, unfazed, puts an arm around my shoulders. I'm grateful for the calming energy.

"He wants to tell me what happened," Mia says calmly, "but he's not upset."

"So it's just me, then?" I ask, laughing nervously.

"Relax. He's coming back to Rosamie's with us."

"Neat!" Terra exclaims, taking the news like we just told her she's getting a puppy.

"How are we going to explain this? How am I supposed to tell Ryan?" I ask without taking a breath.

"Let me find out if we even have to tell him," Mia answers. "It's not like anyone is going to believe us."

"Oh, Ryan will believe us," Terra says, beaming. "Well, he'll believe Emerald, anyway."

It doesn't make me feel any better.

Before we have to explain why we're having a secret meeting, we break our huddle and return to the van.

To our surprise, Ryan has relinquished the driver's seat to Cheddar and now sits at one end of the middle seat. "I've done enough driving for one day," he smiles to me as Mia and Terra climb into the back, leaving plenty of space between them for our new, invisible travel companion.

Even considering my life so far, it's hard not to be a little weirded out sitting right in front of a ghost and right behind the guy who may or may not have made him one. But Mia smiles and giggles for almost the entire ride back to the old plantation. Wyatt must be a real charmer.

Colin notices her laughter and, after casting a few sideways glances at her, he smiles.

Ryan notices too. "Nothing like time on the water to put everyone in a good mood," he grins.

"Sure," Mia humors him. "We'll go with that."

Now I realize it isn't just the warm breeze coming through the van windows, and Mia laughing at Wyatt's inaudible stories, that has everyone so contented. Terra's joyful vibrations fill the van, releasing the last of any tensions we've had to keep bottled up over the course of the day.

Without thinking, I reach out and take Ryan's hand. He looks down in surprise at his hand in mine, then up at me, and smiles.

Back at the plantation, after another of Rosamie's amazing meals and saying goodnight to Ryan and Colin, the girls and I take a walk with Wyatt. The sun dips low in the sky, only slightly cooling the evening air as tree swallows chirp and chatter quietly, settling in for the night.

Mia's having so much fun talking to Wyatt, I'm more than a little jealous. "He loves it here," she smiles. "Rosamie wouldn't let him on the property when he was alive. He says it's almost worth it."

"Ask him what happened to him," says Terra.

"He can hear you, remember?" Mia listens for a few moments, saying "Aw" from time to time as we walk. "He and Colin were deep in the swamp, under a full moon," she tells us. "They were using a spell in the book to try and send Colin back in time. Colin wanted to save his and Ryan's mother, even if he had to give up his own life."

"Aw," Terra interjects.

"Go on," I say, shushing Terra.

"Wyatt says going back in time is impossible. But Colin wouldn't listen. He was blinded by his desire to save his mom. And Wyatt says…." Trailing off, Mia stops walking and looks down at the ground.

The rest of us stop, too. "Well?" I ask. "What does he say?"

"He says it's the same reason Eva wanted the book: to go back in time and be the mother she should have been."

Terra and I stare at her. Something creeps into Mia's eyes—a softness I haven't seen in months. Maybe the ice that encases her heart will thaw after all. Her eyes glisten, but no tears fall. Terra reaches out and gently smoothes her twin's hair.

We resume our walk as Mia continues. "He says that while Colin was trying to conjure up his ticket to the past, Madame DéSolé and some of her brainwashed followers ambushed them. He says she's the only one who wants the book for a practical reason. The book isn't what it seems."

"What *is* anymore?" I say with more sarcasm than intended.

"Colin took the book and ran in one direction; Wyatt took off in another. The trees and shrubs and moss became so thick, he got disoriented. He took a turn when he should have kept straight, and the black waters swallowed him up."

We walk in somber silence for a while, hardly able to conceive of such a frightening or hideous way to die. We step across fallen magnolia petals and it seems a sin to walk on something once so perfect and beautiful. On the ground wilted and browning, no longer blooming proudly, they'll disintegrate and find a new job feeding the earth. I try not to imagine Wyatt drowning, serving a new purpose under the water. Feeding the earth himself.

"Colin thinks he accidentally sent Wyatt back in time instead of himself," Mia goes on. "He thinks he can use the book to bring him back. So he hid the book at his grandmother's house to come back for it once DéSolé's followers were off his track. But Eva found it first, and she found the notes he'd written to himself in the margins. She thought this could be a chance to fix her *own* mistakes."

I rub my temples, which have started to throb. "What a mess."

Terra places one hand on the back of my neck and I feel the pain melt away under her touch. It's faster and more effective than aspirin.

"Everyone has an agenda they can't complete," Mia muses. "Except, perhaps, for DéSolé. Wyatt says she isn't interested in the spells at all. She's looking for directions of some kind."

I sigh. "Great: one more mystery to solve."

"It'll be an adventure!" Terra squeals, bouncing on her toes.

"Wyatt says you've got the right spirit," says Mia. "No pun intended."

"I can't see him, but I can feel him," Terra says, then yells, "Wyatt Breslin, you're all right!"

Mia winces. "Terra, he's dead—not deaf."

Though I've avoided showing it, I'm dying to know what's in the book. The mystery of what DéSolé wants with it is one thing, but the prospect of reading it for myself to solve the mystery of its contents is plenty to send my imagination into high gear. "So what's the plan?" I ask everyone present, including the one I can't see.

Mia's quiet for a moment, listening. I hope Wyatt's got some ideas, because I'm at a loss. I don't know where to find Eva or the book, or how to avoid Madame DéSolé while we look.

"Great," Mia says, sounding thoroughly displeased with Wyatt's answer. "He says Colin knows Eva's regular haunts and that I have to work with him to find her. I also have to be the one to tell Colin that Wyatt is dead and release him from the guilt he feels."

"You're the girl for the job," Terra says, wrapping her arms around Mia and touching foreheads. "And, just maybe, you can do the same for Eva. Her guilt and your anger are a bad combination," she adds, smoothing Mia's hair away from her face and cupping her cheek.

Mia gives her a halfhearted smile, and I can tell she's still struggling to forgive our birth mother. "First things first," she says, then takes a deep breath and exhales. "All right, Wyatt. I'll help Colin find peace on one condition: you stay with me every step of the way." She spits in her right hand and extends it, appearing to shake hands with empty air. It's a deal.

It's also sort of gross to watch.

Night has completely fallen. The darkness is heavy, like layers of black velvet. My eyes ache with fatigue as I struggle to keep them open. I'm so tired I can't think straight and all I want to do is sleep.

I'm not the only one who wants to curl up for the night; Miracle appears and meows in protest of any further conversation. Terra kneels down, and the cat closes her huge green eyes as Terra scratches her behind the ears. Miracle's usually watching, almost as though she'll report back to Rosamie on all our activities. But tonight, she seems content to convince us to come to bed.

"Tell Wyatt we say goodnight," Terra says.

"Again, Terra—dead, not deaf," says Mia with a sleepy smile. "He can hear everything you say. He'll keep an eye on things tonight. And, Terra?"

"Yeah?"

"Wyatt says, 'Sweet dreams, loud girl.' "

With Miracle leading the way, we head to our guest house.

After opening a window to let in the cool night breeze, we climb into our beds. Our green-eyed friend curls up in her favorite spot, behind Mia's knees. The night is alive with a chorus of crickets and frogs, singing and croaking so loudly, you'd think sleep would be impossible. But I'm out before my head hits the pillow.

I wake the next morning to someone tapping on our door. The twins are still sound asleep and Miracle snores softly. As I open the door a crack, I see Rosamie standing there with a deep purple sky behind her.

"You're up before the sun," I say.

She's fully dressed and looks wide awake. "Indeed, I am. Do me a blessing, will you? Come and keep me company over coffee."

"Sure," I answer quietly. "Let me throw on some clothes. I'll be right up."

As much as I'd like to crawl back into bed, I can tell Rose wants to talk to me. She's not the kind of person who always needs company, especially at oh-dark-thirty in the morning.

After throwing on jeans and a sweater, I try rousing Miracle to see if she wants to join me. She just stretches and burrows herself further under Mia's leg. "Suit yourself," I whisper. Miracle twitches her tail in reply but never opens her eyes.

Slipping out the cottage door to make my way to the main house, hundreds of birds are singing and chattering as the sun's first rays break through the palm trees to the east. This place is so different from Santa Cruz, where most mornings are foggy and the air heavy with sea salt. Here, the breeze carries the perfume of the garden's orange tree and rich earth as the morning sun warms them. Yet it seems no matter where I am, water isn't far off. I like it that way.

The smell of coffee and sweet rolls welcomes me as I walk into the kitchen, where Rose sits at the table arranging a bouquet of flowers in a vase of pale-purple glass. "Get yourself some coffee and a sweet roll. Your friend Cheddar will be along in no time and your sisters will be fortunate if there's anything left at all."

"You know him well," I say as I take a seat at the table.

"He's got a good soul, Emerald. But you know that." Rose smiles as she pulls one flower from its spot, meticulously places it somewhere else, and turns the vase this way and that, eyeing the new arrangement from every side. "As a rule, you surround yourself with kind-hearted people. You keep them near and dear. Correct?"

"Try to." I cup my hands around my mug of coffee. "My sisters do, too."

"But one who was supposed to stay near, did not. You want to know why." Rosamie has wasted no time in revealing the subject of our early-morning meeting.

"Of course I want to know."

Finally satisfied with the flowers, Rose slides the vase to the middle of the table. She sits back and folds her hands in her lap, directing her eyes at me. "My dear, the destiny of rain is to fall. It has no choice; it's in its nature to do so. Some people, as much as we'd like to believe otherwise, have no choice in the things they do. That's nature, too. *Their* nature. Whether by fate or a fault of their own, they choose a path that makes no sense to most folk."

I can tell it's not the time to respond. I wouldn't know what to say, anyway. I just sip my coffee and nibble on my gooey cinnamon roll.

"Child, keep this truth tucked in your heart, as it's the most honest thing I can tell you. If your heart is good… and I know yours is, mind you… when someone hurts you, it has everything to do with them and very little to do with you. Now, I'm not saying you should lie down like a doormat and let people walk all over you. Not at all. What I'm saying is, the damage people inflict—whether they be enemies or your own kin—comes from their own broken places. You didn't cause it, you didn't deserve it, but you do need to try to understand it and offer as much forgiveness as you can. Refusing to forgive another is no different than stabbing yourself and expecting the other person to bleed."

"So you think we should forgive Eva?" I ask quietly.

"I do," Rose says with an assured nod. "Maybe not today, or next week, but certainly before it's too late. And no living soul on this good, green earth knows when 'too late' is coming until it's already passed."

"Terra's already forgiven her. I can too, I think. She was so young when she had us. I can't imagine wanting to be a mom for another... I don't know, a long time." I sip my coffee. It's not every day I talk with an almost-stranger about how old I think I'll be when making a baby becomes a viable life choice. But I like Rose, almost-stranger or no. "Mia's a different story. That's going to be tough for her," I add, getting up to freshen both of our coffees.

"Oh, I wouldn't worry too much about Mia," says Rose with a wry smile. "You three girls seem to attract all kinds of help. I'm confident that before this is all said and done, her heart will undergo a softening."

Before I can find out what Rose is hinting at, the back door opens. Miracle slinks in, followed by Cheddar and the girls. The cat heads straight for the bowl of smoked salmon that Rose has set out for her; Cheddar heads straight for the sweet rolls.

"Well, that does it," Rose says with a defeated laugh. "I'll have to put another batch in the oven before Ryan and Colin get here."

Cheddar holds a plate of rolls above Terra, a good two feet out of reach, as he asks, "What's the plan for today?"

"We're going into the French Quarter to look for costumes for Halloween," I say as I hand Terra my plate with the last precious roll.

"Oh, you all won't find anything good to wear in the Quarter," Rosamie says, "unless you want to look like all the other girls with feather masks and Mardi Gras beads. If you want some real costumes, go on up to the attic and have a look around."

If it involves clothes, you don't have to tell a Tempest girl twice. Just as soon as the offer leaves Rose's mouth, the twins and I are heading up the stairs to the attic.

The top floor of the house is dark and stuffy. Mia lights an oil lamp, bathing the attic in a ghostly, flickering glow. Wooden crates and chests of varying sizes line the walls. Dresses and long jacquard topcoats hang from bars fastened to exposed beams. Lacey hats and plumed tricorns rest atop piles of corsets and sashes.

"Looks like *Pirates of the Caribbean* in here," Mia says, surveying the bounty.

"Aye," says Terra, who's already thrown on a wide, brown leather belt and wears an unbuckled, deep-red corset over her shirt like a vest. She tops it off with a pirate's hat. "Someone let Johnny Depp know he's not getting his clothes back!"

"It's not Depp you need to worry about, Terra," Mia cautions. "A couple of the original owners of these clothes are watching, and they don't look too happy."

"Not to be rude, but they've already had a lifetime to party." Terra frowns. "Not that they lived nearly as long as we do now."

"Median life expectancy was around thirty," I offer. Freshman year, while helping the school librarians, I became obsessed with an entire shelf's worth of smelly old vital-statistics almanacs.

Mia glances at the grumbling ghosts. "Right on the money, I'd say."

Terra, beaming, addresses the corner where Mia's looking. "See? You made out pretty well!"

"Um—" I venture, "it was around thirty because there were so many awful and gross ways to die that science didn't have a handle on yet."

Terra shoots me a dirty look. "Thanks. Big help." Turning to the corner, she tries again. "Look—we promise to avoid mud puddles, and no spaghetti, and we'll return every little thing exactly as we found it. Right, ladies?"

"Absolutely," I promise; Mia covers her heart and raises her other hand in a silent pledge.

Soon she tells us the young couple…the old couple?…the *dead* couple is satisfied, and they've gone to haunt the master bedroom.

"I have to admit," I giggle, pulling a dress off the rack, "I love the idea of wearing an authentic outfit for Halloween. Mia, help me pull this dress tight in the back." The deep-green satin dress has cream-colored lace lining a square neckline, three-quarter sleeves cuffed with the same lace, and, even through a couple centuries' worth of wear and tear, lights up my eyes like fireworks. The hemline brushes the floor, and waves of emerald green flow around my legs.

Mia comes to look over my shoulder at my reflection. "You look perfect. Now take a deep breath and let it *aaall* the way out," she orders.

As I do, she pulls the satin ribbon in the back and tightens the bodice so fast I can't take any air back in. "*Mia!*" I squeak.

"Hey, you want authentic, right? You're lucky you didn't put on one of those herringbone corsets. You'd be passed out like a proper lady in no time," Mia cackles. Still, she shows mercy and loosens the ribbon enough for me to breathe.

For herself, Mia finds a deep-blue, velvet dress with black lace trim. She coils her hair into an elegant swirl on top of her head and ties it with a black satin ribbon with ends hanging just below her collarbone.

Terra joins us at the mirror as we admire ourselves. "Em, look," she says, holding out a pendant on a white-gold chain. A stunningly large, rectangular emerald surrounded by diamonds sparkles in the lamplight.

"It's perfect," I say.

"Hold up your hair," Terra says; I do, and she fastens the clasp behind my neck. She finger-combs my hair and pulls it to one side, forming a loose braid that cascades over my right shoulder.

As we stand shoulder to shoulder, viewing our reflections in the mirror, I feel as though I'm lost in fairytale. I wonder if the people that Mia sees feel this way, as though the past and the future don't exist and the only reality is the brilliant and beautiful now.

"Yep, this is *way* better than plastic Mardi Gras beads," Mia announces.

"I'd say so." I gently touch the emerald that rests just above the lace trim of my collar.

"Well, now," Rosamie says from the top of the stairs, "you can wear the dress to the Quarter—but not the necklace."

"Oh—I'm sorry," I stammer, unclasping it. I didn't hear her come up; I don't think any of us did. "It was just so beautiful, I tried it on."

Rose steps into the room. "You can try it on any time you like. It's been handed down in our family for generations," she says wistfully. "The last person to wear it was Ryan's mother. It looks beautiful on you. I'm sure she would approve."

"Thank you," I say quietly as I hand the necklace back to Rosamie.

"It's just that, while no one there tomorrow night is likely to rip that dress off of you, they most certainly would give this necklace a go." Rose smiles, placing the pendant back in its box. "There's a parade tomorrow night and you girls will want to walk in it. We have plenty of cousins who work the floats, so be sure you get down to the Quarter early and keep the boys close, just to be safe. Most people are out for good fun on Halloween, but you're never too far from danger in the darker corners and side streets."

I cast a glance at Mia, who raises her eyebrows. She knows all too well what to watch for.

Just as Rosamie heads down the stairs, Ryan comes bounding up. "Hey now, what's going on up here?" he asks, appraising our costumes.

I smile. "What do you think?"

"I think I'm going to have to do better than the orange T-shirt with the word COSTUME printed on the front that I planned to wear." He takes my hands in his and, after fully taking in the dress, his gaze trails up the length of my braid, finally meeting my eyes. "Wow," he says, shaking his head. "Colin and Cheddar will have to step up their games, too. No way are we going to let you three have all the fun."

"Deal. But for now, I'm melting," I say, fairly sure I'm going to pass out if I don't change. "We'll be down in a few minutes."

"Yes, ma'am." Ryan bows and turns on his heels.

The girls and I hurry to change, being careful to hang the dresses just as we found them, minding our promise to their original owners.

When we come down the stairs, Colin has arrived; he, Ryan, Rosamie and Cheddar stand around the kitchen table, looking at us in silence.

"That's about the reaction I was going for," says Mia, striking a glamour pose.

"I don't think it's us," I tell her, reading the grave looks on their faces. Colin's jaw is set with grim determination. "What is it?" I ask.

He answers, "I know where Eva is."

CHAPTER
5

THE IDEA OF FINALLY CONFRONTING Eva completely destroys the fun of trying on costumes and thinking about Halloween. A friend of Colin's saw her waiting tables at a music club called the Spotted Cat. Riding in silence, I'm sure each of us is playing out a different scenario in their head—each with an agenda, each with a hoped-for outcome. I can't think past getting the book back and ending the drama surrounding it. I'm sure Colin feels the same. Mia, on the other side of the coin, is probably thinking about ways to make sure Eva understands even a portion of the hurt she's carried since learning the truth.

As we reach Frenchmen Street, the tension hangs thick like humidity. With no plan, I'm nervous about even talking to Eva without scaring her away and having to start the search all over again.

Ryan can tell I'm on edge and offers to go into the club first. "There's no sense in ambushing her," he says as the rest of us wait a few doors down.

The noon heat is impressive for late October, but dark clouds in the distance hint at a storm on the way. Terra hums a barely audible tune, but I can tell she's trying to calm everyone down. It's certainly working on Cheddar, as he happily studies a menu on the door of a little sandwich shop. Mia and Colin both stand utterly still, arms crossed, with eyes fixed on the club door.

Ryan walks out with his hands in his pockets, shaking his head. I realize I've been holding my breath and that I'm more than a little relieved for the delay in reuniting with Eva. "She's not there, but the bartender says she works this afternoon. We've got time to kill," he says, putting an arm around my shoulders. "Relax, Em. We're close."

We walk along Frenchmen Street, enjoying the sight of people already in costume. "They've been celebrating for days," Ryan says as some people with dogs in costume walk past us. A four-legged clown and a devil prance ahead as a dachshund in a rubber hot-dog bun tries to keep up. The dachshund's owners are dressed as ketchup and mustard bottles. Clever. "But tomorrow night is the real show," Ryan adds, smiling as the dogs pass.

The idea of celebrating Halloween with so much color and intensity excites me. On an average day, the streets of New Orleans are already abuzz with history and ghosts of their own; they're the perfect place to blur the line between fantasy and reality.

Just as I'm about to ask Ryan about his costume plans for tomorrow, I see Colin cross the street ahead of us, approaching a group of people standing in front of a small shop with shuttered doors and a distressed wooden overhang atop the entrance. Elaborately decorated skeletons and voodoo dolls hang in the windows between thick, purple velvet drapes.

The group, mostly teenage boys, stares in our direction. There's a vacancy in their eyes that makes me uneasy. Three of them close around Colin as another two sit on the steps in front of the shop, as though guarding it. Their clothes are a mix of dingy white long-sleeve shirts, V-neck tees, and loose pants. The boys surrounding Colin seem to plead with him, but Colin shakes his head.

Ryan stops in his tracks. "Hang on."

The rest of us crowd alongside him. "What's up?" Cheddar asks, eyeing the group as Colin talks to them in low tones.

"Those are Madame DéSolé's people, and that shop sells Voodoo supplies. We need to keep our distance."

"They don't look much older than we are," Mia says.

"They're not. DéSolé preys on kids who are lost or in trouble. It's how she roped Colin in."

"Easy prey." Cheddar shakes his head in disgust.

I study the group from a distance. No one smiles, and the conversation grows heated. In under a minute, Colin makes his way back to us, his face flushed with anger. "DéSolé wants to meet with me. I'm going, but it's better if the rest of you don't."

"I'm not sure that's a good idea," Ryan says.

Colin holds Ryan in his gaze. "Only one way to find out."

The group across the street stares in our direction. Even with Ryan and Cheddar next to us, I feel vulnerable.

"They know where we're staying," Terra whispers. "The same group was watching us the night we got to Rosamie's. I'd recognize that vibration anywhere."

Mia nods anxiously. "And the white clothes."

I expect Colin to dismiss Mia, but instead, his face softens. "Nothing will happen to you there. Even DéSolé's crew won't mess with Rosamie, or set foot on her property."

Without thinking, Terra interrupts, "They *can't* set foot on it. It's protected."

All three boys turn and look at her as though she just proclaimed she's running for Mayor of Crazy Town. "Now, what would make you say that?" Ryan asks.

"She's just agreeing with you," Mia answers. "As in, Rosamie wouldn't let anything happen."

"Sure," Ryan says, unconvinced.

"Look, I'm going," Colin says, growing impatient. "I'll meet you all back here in a couple of hours." To Mia he adds, "It'll be fine. I promise."

We watch as Colin returns to his so-called friends and they all move up the street in a tight cluster, vanishing into the crowd. Mia leans over to me and whispers, "Wyatt's going with him."

I smile, fully realizing the advantages our unseen tagalong affords us. No matter what happens, with Wyatt there to listen in and watch their every move, we'll get the real story.

We walk a bit more and, after picking up a few Cheddar-approved sandwiches, we find a wooded park with plenty of shade to picnic in while waiting. The twins and I are only halfway through our sandwiches when Cheddar finishes and falls asleep. Ryan follows suit, the satisfaction of a full stomach and a sun-dappled autumn afternoon making a nap all but impossible to resist.

Resting under the trees, I feel safe again. Not because of Cheddar and Ryan, but because of my sisters. As menacing as DéSolé's group was, here with Mia and Terra, I feel powerful. Being near them in this peaceful place reminds me just how much we're capable of.

I look over at Ryan, the front of his white T-shirt gently rising and falling with each breath. He's on his home turf and looks as relaxed as you'd expect.

Out of the blue, Terra remarks, "It's special here. There are so many vibrations, layered one on top of the other. I can feel the Mississippi River moving along the waterfront…people walking through the streets…and every conversation happening at once. There's sadness and joy. It all blends together—like music."

Mia, getting fidgety, throws a piece of bread at me to get my attention. "Hey, speed things up a bit," she says in as loud a whisper as she dares. "I can't wait any more."

Putting my finger to my lips to shush her, I nod my head in agreement. Cheddar and Ryan should be none the wiser when they come out of their siesta.

I close my eyes and lean my head back, breathing in deeply. My body relaxes, and I ground myself to the earth beneath me. As I exhale, I push time forward.

Hours turn to minutes; minutes to seconds. People stroll by at the speed of Olympic runners; lunch-hour traffic looks like a NASCAR event; and little white clouds, their shapes constantly changing, gently race across the sky.

Just as I begin slowing time back down, I realize with horror that I've allowed myself to become distracted by our surroundings. I don't know how long Ryan's eyes have been open, but they're open so wide, I think they might fall out of his head as he looks around at the decelerating world around us.

As time resumes its normal pace, he raises himself up on one elbow with a look of mounting alarm. "What just happened?"

I look to Mia and Terra, but they're both staring right back at me with horrified expressions. I imagine my own expression is more or less a match.

"Can we talk about it later?" My brain whirs away in search of a simple explanation.

"So you saw it, too. I didn't just dream that?"

I mentally kick myself, realizing too late that such an explanation might have satisfied him. "No," I tell him.

Mia begins to interject—to tell Ryan I'm short a few marbles, and she didn't see a thing, and whatever *he* saw was totally a dream—but Terra puts a hand on her shoulder and shakes her head gravely, as if to say what my heart knows is true: it's too late for another lie. If we get in the habit of telling Ryan he's misread his own senses, soon enough he'll start thinking he's lost *his* marbles. That would be cruel and unfair to him, and it would be our fault.

Terra's smart like that. She's almost always the first to think of these things.

"No," I say with more assurance. "You didn't dream it."

Ryan gets up, brushing the grass from his jeans. "So…you know what it was?"

I nod, barely able to meet his gaze.

The next thing I hear from him is a chuckle, which is so *not* the reaction I expected that I have to look at him to assess whether his marbles have already vacated the premises. But no—the alarm is gone from his face, replaced by a twinkle in his eyes that makes me want to laugh too. "Things are never boring with you three," he says, and goes to nudge Cheddar with his foot, but not before adding, "I look forward to an explanation once we've done what we're here to do."

At the touch of Ryan's boot, Cheddar opens his eyes and sits up with a stretch and a roaring yawn. "How long was I out?"

Checking the time on his phone, Ryan answers, "About an hour. Give or take." He directs that last part at me, smiling quizzically.

And with that, he's all business again. Once Cheddar's fully awake and upright, we make our way back to the Spotted Cat. There's still no sign of Colin, but we can't put off our reunion with Eva any longer.

The club is dimly lit, its cool air a stark contrast to the heat and humidity of the park. As the front door closes behind us, we scan the room for Eva amongst the scattered patrons.

Eyes adjusting to the dim, I spot her standing at the end of the bar, chatting with the bartender. He notices us first and motions toward us, and Eva turns our way. Clearly expecting customers, shock washes over her face as recognition dawns. She recovers quickly as she makes her way over to us. It's a relief to finally be getting this moment over with, but most of us appear to have no idea what to say, so we hang back.

Terra's the exception. She goes straight to Eva and hugs her. "Hi, Mom." Eva closes her eyes, hugging her tightly in return.

Terra's done nothing to change the tense vibrations of the situation for the rest of us. And, honestly—I'm grateful for it. We can't charm our way through all of life's awkward meetings. Courage has to be learned in real time. We all need to feel everything that's happening in this moment, and Terra doesn't interfere.

She lets go of our mother and offers a genuine smile.

Mia, keeping her distance, says simply, "Hello, Eva."

One *Mom* and one *Eva*. Great—I'm the tiebreaker. I manage a smile. "Hey."

"You girls are a long way from home. What are you doing here?" Eva asks, trying to sound unaffected.

"You know exactly why we're here," Mia says sharply, getting right to the point. "Where is the book?"

Eva immediately goes on the defense. "The book is none of your business, Mia."

"You made it our business when you brought it to Santa Cruz, didn't you?" Mia replies, her anger boiling over. "You took something that never belonged to you, and put all of us at risk."

Eva takes a step toward Mia, prompting Ryan and Cheddar to close in. "You don't know anything about it. Don't come to my work making accusations."

Mia tries to take a step toward Eva, but Cheddar stops her. Seeing the bartender's concerned look, Ryan places himself between Mia and Eva and tries to calm them down. "Let's not do this here. We just want to find the book. You can resolve your family issues another time, and in a better place."

"Eva's spent her entire life avoiding family issues," Mia scoffs.

Eva's eyes harden. "Get out," she says through clenched teeth.

"Fine." Mia turns on her heels and walks out the front door of the club with Cheddar following close behind.

Desperate to salvage our chance at finding the book, I plead with Eva, "Can we just sit down for a minute and talk?"

Terra finally steps in, placing her arm around Eva, who quickly calms under the influence of her charm. She knows what Terra's doing—how could she not?—but lets her do it anyway, probably realizing it's necessary to avoid making a scene. "Okay," she says quietly. "Just for a minute."

"Eva—Mom—please, we just want to get the book back where it belongs," I say, trying not to place blame. "It's been with Ryan's family for generations and it's really important we return it." I look around. A few patrons have taken interest in our conversation but look away as I meet their eyes. Lowering my voice, I add, "There are other people looking for it, too. Dangerous people."

"Madame DéSolé," says Eva. "I know all about her. Her people have been watching me since I came back. But why does she want it?"

Not sure how to answer, I look to Ryan.

"We don't know, Ms. Tempest, but we want to find it first and deal with her afterward. Your daughters are in danger until we get the book back," he says, his eyes steady, his voice gentle but firm. "Where are you staying?"

Eva studies Ryan for a moment, gauging his trustworthiness perhaps, then answers cautiously. "I have an apartment at the Saint Philip. I don't keep the book there, but give me a couple of days, and I'll help you."

"Deal," Ryan says, and reaches his hand out to her. She shakes it, but I'm still not entirely convinced we can count on her. I can't stand feeling that way about my own birth mother. I doubt she feels great about it, either.

Terra senses my concern and speaks up. "Mom, if you do help us, it'll go a long way toward healing Mia's heart. You want that, don't you?"

"I don't think anything is going to get her to stop hating me," Eva says, her eyes downcast.

"That's not true," Terra says, rubbing Eva's arm. "It's just going to take time. Consider returning the book a first step."

"Maybe once we get it back, we can talk about, you know—everything else," I add.

There's sadness in her eyes, but tenderness too, as she looks from me to Terra and back. "I know you girls have questions. I will answer them."

"When?" I ask.

The bartender calls Eva's name, pointing to a tray of drinks that aren't going to serve themselves.

"Coming," Eva calls, then looks from the bartender to us and softly tells us, "Soon. I pr—" She catches herself, instantly ashamed. "I don't suppose my promises mean much to you."

I can't stand it any longer. Whatever she's called now, I hug her tight, and don't let go until I feel Terra tugging my sleeve. We don't want to get Eva in trouble.

I want to tell her *Te quiero*, "I love you," but I can't. Not yet. I still don't truly know this woman who's been in and out of our lives for as far back as I can remember. I still don't understand the choices she made. Maybe we'll get some answers in two days; that's when we agree to meet her again.

Gray clouds hang in the distance when we step out into the heat, leaving Eva to her work. We cross the street to where Cheddar and Mia wait for us. Both have ice cream—a wise move on Cheddar's part; Mia needed cooling down. Though the sun hangs low in the sky, we see no sign of Colin.

"Well, how'd it go?" Cheddar asks.

"We're going to her place the day after tomorrow to get the book," says Ryan, sounding more confident than

I feel. "I want to get you all back to the plantation and then I'll see if I can track Colin down."

Mia never takes her eyes off her ice cream, but all the same, I can tell she doesn't believe for a second that any of us will see Eva in two days.

"Let's get going," Ryan says.

"Can we stop and pick up beignets for Rosamie?" Cheddar asks.

Ryan pats Cheddar's belly. "For Rosamie, huh?"

After stopping at Café DuMonde, we head back to the plantation. The ride is quiet and I'm sure Ryan is going over the day's events in his mind—specifically, the part where everything around us was in fast forward for no apparent reason. I'm not exactly sure how to answer the questions he'll ask, but we've come too far in our journey for me to keep the truth of our charms from him much longer.

Back at Laurent Plantation, the twins, Cheddar, and the beignets head into Rosamie's house. Ryan doesn't follow and I know it's time to talk. "Care to walk?" he asks, offering a hand.

I take it without saying anything and we stroll toward the back of the property. The sky is clear, the stars just beginning to come out. Croaking frogs and chirring crickets fill the silence between us.

We come to a bench under a magnolia tree, surrounded by jasmine that's just starting to bloom in the warm night air. Sitting down, Ryan turns to face me, taking my hand. "So, today, in the park?"

I turn my head to the side, scrunching my nose a bit. "Is this a *want* to know thing, or a *need* to know thing?"

A wide, warm smile crosses his face. "You know, Em, I've seen a lot of strange things growing up here. Some have a cut-and-dry explanation and some don't. But whatever your explanation is, I hope you know you can trust me with it."

The air is suddenly heavy with expectation. I glance this way and that, searching for the right words. Nothing but darkness in every direction.

As far as I know, nobody outside of our family has ever been entrusted with the secret of our charms. Now I'm faced with either sharing the truth or continuing to hide it. Each choice comes at a cost.

I decide that at the very least, I can share *my* secret. Mia and Terra can decide for themselves if, and how much, they want to share. "I was born with a unique gift. It runs in my family, on the women's side."

He says nothing; he just keeps my hand in his and listens intently.

"If I need to, in certain situations, I can slow down, or speed up, the passage of time. It's not witchcraft, and it's not an illusion. It's the ability to manipulate physics."

Ryan slouches into the bench's backrest and looks up at the sky, but doesn't let go of my hand. "Wow."

I let it sink in a bit. I've lived with this knowledge all my life; I can't imagine what it's like to hear it for the first time, or how crazy I probably sound.

He takes in a deep breath, then lets it out, and I wonder if he's decided to count the stars, because he's been silent for a few moments now.

"Wow good, or wow bad?" I ask carefully.

He looks down from the sky to me, and smiles. "Wow incredible."

I study him for any sign of sarcasm, then laugh like a dork because it feels like a ten-ton weight just fell off my shoulders. "Oh. Good."

"The first time I saw you, I knew there was something different about you. Something special."

"And now you know what it is," I say, remembering the bonfire on the beach in Santa Cruz. It feels like years ago in some ways, and like right now in other ways, and it makes me smile so big it kind of hurts.

"No, Em, that isn't it. I mean, it's amazing. But it's not what makes you special. Not to me, I mean. The way your eyes catch the light; the way you smile when you're reading a book; the way you laugh with your sisters; your intelligence; your bravery; your loyalty—there's so much more to you than the time thing. I notice new stuff every day."

I'm at a loss for words. The nicest compliment I ever get from boys back home is, "You're pretty." To hear someone detail qualities they like about you is both wonderful and strange. At the moment, I can't articulate the things I feel about him, and it doesn't seem like the right moment anyway.

"What about your sisters? The way the three of you interact, I'm guessing you aren't the only one with this power."

"That's their story to tell. When the time is right, you can ask them. For now, you'll have to settle for mine. And you've got to keep it to yourself."

"Of course. I'd tell you that you can trust me, but I'm pretty sure at least one of you Tempest girls can tell if I'm true to my word," he laughs.

"That's right. And if you're not, you'll find out the hard way which one of us it is."

"I'm not tempting fate," he says with a wink.

I look up to find that clouds have blotted out the stars. The air is still warm and fragrant, but it smells like rain.

"Tomorrow is Halloween," Ryan remarks. "I know my cousin's got your costumes covered. I'll pick you up at four and take you and your sisters to the French Quarter for the parade. Today was awkward, and the day after tomorrow's probably going to be weirder still. Might as well have fun while we can, right?"

"What about Colin?" I ask. "Why do you think he hasn't come back?"

"He's good for that. He'll disappear for a couple of days at a time. I'll find him. I always do."

I hope he's right. We just found Eva; we're closer than ever to getting the book back. The last thing we need is to lose the person who wants it back most of all.

"He's not a bad person, Em. He's just broken in so many places. But since we met you and your sisters, I've seen him changing. Not all at once, mind you, and he's constantly on the verge of falling back on his old ways. But I've seen it. Especially with Mia. He's different around her. He puts on a good show, but I think he has a thing for her."

"We've come to pretty much the same conclusion," I say, sighing. "In the van. He kept looking at her—weird and not weird at the same time" I watch the expanse of clouds roll by over our heads. "It would have been better if he'd had a thing for Terra," I sigh, almost to myself.

"Well, we don't get to choose who we fall for," he says, brushing the hair away from my eyes.

I feel myself blush and I'm glad the night is so dark.

"Maybe they'd be good for each other," he offers.

"Or a complete train wreck."

"Let's hope not. We have enough of a mess to sort through as it is." He stands up, my hand still in his, pulling me up from the bench. "I'll walk you back to the main house." He pulls a sprig of jasmine from its vine and tucks it into my hair, just over my ear.

As we walk toward the house, he begins to slow and stops me just before the steps to Rosamie's kitchen. He looks at me for a moment, as if trying to decide what to say. Finally he says, "Thank you for trusting me, Emerald Tempest." He leans down, his face just over mine, and just as he's about to kiss my cheek, a cold, fat raindrop splashes me in one eye.

"Nice," I say loudly, my eye furiously blinking of its own accord. The moment's officially broken.

We look up to the sky as the sound of raindrops on palm leaves and cobblestones gets really loud, really fast. "Either I have the worst timing ever, or somebody's trying to tell me something," Ryan laughs, almost having to shout over the downpour.

"You're entitled to a do-over," I smile, and instantly feel my cheeks flush. "See you tomorrow."

I run up the steps and into the house. Rosamie has gone to bed and the house is softly lit by just a few lamps. Cheddar's asleep again in the living room, just a smudge of powdered sugar on the front of his shirt, rising and falling as he snores. *His manners are improving*, I think with a smile, already over the worst of my embarrassment.

Mia and Terra are drinking tea at the kitchen table. "Did you guys save me a beignet?" I ask hopefully.

"We did, but it wasn't easy," Terra answers. "He eats so fast, I'm pretty sure some of them ended up in his lungs."

Laughing, I join them at the table. Just as I take my first bite, Mia asks with a sly smile, "So, how was your chat with Ryan?"

Taking in a breath to answer, I inhale powdered sugar and cough for almost a minute, making it look like I'm stalling. Terra slides her tea toward me. "It was interesting," I answer matter-of-factly once I've had a sip of Terra's tea and the spasms have subsided.

"Share a secret or two, did we?" Mia presses with a grin.

I put down my beignet and stare at her. "How do you know?"

She shrugs. "In addition to being dead, and very funny, Wyatt is also very nosy."

CHAPTER
6

ONCE I'VE ASSURED MIA AND TERRA that I only shared the truth of my own charm with Ryan, and the details of the near-kiss derailed by rain, Mia relays what Wyatt learned from Colin's visit with Madame DéSolé. "She told Colin that she'll conjure a spell to bring Wyatt back. Colin wants so badly to believe her, he promised to bring her the book as soon as he has it. Wyatt calls her a crafty shrew who'll say anything to get what she wants."

"We'll have to tell him the truth," I say. "If we don't, every action he takes will be for the wrong reason."

Mia shakes her head. "He'll never believe it."

"We have to find a way to prove it to him," says Terra, pacing the room in thought.

Mia follows Terra with her eyes. "Any idea how we're supposed to do that?"

"Maybe Wyatt can help us," I suggest.

Terra stops pacing and we watch as Mia listens to

Wyatt. She tells us with a laugh, "He's game. 'Anything to knock DéSolé off her high horse,' he says."

"Ryan and I will meet Eva at her place the day after tomorrow to get the book back; she promised she'd give it to us," I offer, knowing full well that Mia won't trust anything Eva says.

As expected, Mia rolls her eyes. "Do you have a Plan B for when you get there and she's packed up and left?"

Terra takes Mia's hand. "She won't. She'll be there and she'll give the book back. I could feel it. Also, it's actually tomorrow," she adds, pointing to an antique wall clock. It's six minutes past midnight.

Terra hops up and down, beaming. "Happy Halloween!"

"Happy Halloween, and I still don't believe it," Mia says, standing from her chair to stretch her back.

"Let's get Captain Beignet off the couch and into bed," I say as we clean up the teacups. "I'm exhausted."

It's still raining when we step outside and Miracle isn't happy about having to wait for her warm bed with Mia. She paws at Mia's legs, then turns to run down the walkway toward the guest houses. "Ah, rain—the romance killer," Mia says, holding a sweatshirt over her head.

"It's supposed to clear up by tomorrow night," Terra assures us. "Well—tonight, I guess."

"A packed French Quarter on Halloween night sounds like the *real* romance killer," I yawn. "Not really what I had in mind."

We get Cheddar into his room and retreat to the shelter of our own. After slipping under the covers, I try to prep Mia for what's to come with Eva. "Eventually we're going to have to talk with Eva about the past. I don't want to leave New Orleans without some answers."

Mia strokes Miracle's fur as she curls up, happy to be out of the rain and buried in a down comforter. "What will it change, Em? It's not going to erase the past. She made her choice and took away ours. We all have to live with it."

"But maybe hearing what she has to say will make it *easier* to live with. Don't you want to know why she did it?"

"I guess," Mia answers quietly.

Terra sits up in bed. "We should give her a chance. Let her tell her story. Then, we can tell ours. What is there to lose? No matter what, we have each other. Nothing can change that."

"You should write greeting cards," Mia says flatly, then softens. "But, yeah."

As angry as Mia is, I know that somewhere inside her, there's forgiveness. Even if it's just a little bit, our love for her will help her find it. With our support, she'll find a way to be strong. We all will.

We sleep late into the morning and wake to the sound of banging on our door.

"Unless you have coffee, go away," I yell.

"Open the door!" Cheddar yells back, his voice muffled.

"Do you have coffee?" Mia calls out.

"No, but I know where to get some. *Open up!*"

Mia opens it, and standing there, filling almost the entire frame, stands Cheddar in overalls, a battered flannel shirt, and a rubber jack-o'-lantern head mask. "*Raaaah!*" he fake-roars from beneath the mask.

Terra laughs. "What are you supposed to be?"

Cheddar pulls the mask halfway off so that the jack-o'-lantern's scrunched-up face rests on his forehead. "You've seriously never seen a scarecrow?"

"You're missing the 'scare' part," I say, trying to untangle myself from my quilt.

"You don't see any crows around, do you?" Cheddar replies. He's not wrong. "Come on to the main house. Rosamie made pumpkin pancakes and we're going to decorate for a party she's hosting tonight and we'll come back here after we go into the French Quarter." In his excitement, he sounds like a ten-year-old.

"You might want to skip the caffeine today," Mia tells him.

As promised, a late breakfast awaits us. The scents of pumpkin, nutmeg and cinnamon waft through the kitchen, and a large bowl of fluffy whipped cream sits beside a tray of fresh butter.

After eating our fill of pancakes, we help Rosamie decorate. Orange and amber blown-glass pumpkins sit in neat rows, ready to be placed around the house. There are silver trays full of pralines, bright-red candied apples, and carved pumpkins with sugar candles inside, waiting for sunset.

Mia helps Cheddar string purple and gold streamers while Terra places black candleholders on the mantel. Miracle sniffs at a metal statue of a black cat, and deciding it's not a threat to her station as reigning queen, she busies herself trying to undo the progress Mia's made hanging streamers.

Rosamie places orange- and purple-jeweled sugar skulls in between antique silver candleholders and positions a lifelike skeleton with a Mardi Gras mask and an orange feather boa by the front door. "We know how to do it up here, don't we?" she asks, stepping back to admire our work.

"Yes, you do," Cheddar says right before chomping into a candied apple with an impressively loud *crunch!*

"You'd best save the rest of those for the kids, pumpkin-head," she says, moving the tray of apples out of his reach. Turning back to us, she plants her hands on her hips. "The day is slipping away. You girls should get your costumes on before the Laurent boys arrive. I have some costume jewelry you can wear with your dresses, instead of those family heirlooms." She ushers us up to the attic to change.

After helping each other into our costumes and fixing our hair, we admire ourselves in the full-length mirror. "Two proper ladies and a salty pirate girl," Terra says, adjusting her belt and straightening her plumed tricorn hat. Mia and I have our hair pulled back in loose ponytails, but Terra's wild hair flows freely, the perfect picture of pirate chic.

The sun is just setting when we hear a knock at the front door. "Showtime," I say as I clasp a fleur-de-lis cameo necklace behind my neck.

As we descend the stairs, I see Ryan and Colin standing in the foyer. They're dressed in matching Victorian suits, with top hats and long-tailed coats. Ryan wears a puffy, emerald-green satin necktie, perfectly matching my dress; Colin's tie is midnight blue, the same color as Mia's.

"Good evening, ladies," Ryan says, tipping his hat. "Told you I'd find him."

"You found him and you talked him into dressing up. I'm impressed," I answer with a curtsy.

Ryan looks Cheddar up and down, taking in his overalls, skuzzy flannel, and mask. "Let me guess: you're a squash farmer in the witness protection program."

Cheddar's pumpkin head droops defeatedly.

"He's a scarecrow," the girls and I say in unison.

"I knew it," says Ryan, patting Cheddar on the arm. "Just playing with you. We better get going."

"You all be careful down in the quarter," Rosamie calls after us as we make our way to the front door. "There will be plenty of fun, and plenty of scares. You just keep Cheddar close by in case you need to chase someone off," she adds with a wink, and Cheddar seems to cheer up.

As I follow the others out, Rosamie touches my shoulder, holding me back. "Keep this on you, child, close to your heart. It'll keep you safe tonight."

She presses a small pouch made of what looks like rattlesnake skin into my palm; opening it, I find a silver pendant with Saint Michael the Archangel engraved on the front and the words PROTECT US on the back.

"Don't take any unnecessary risks," Rose advises me. "But should trouble find you, don't forget you have that."

I do as she advises, tucking the medal into the bodice of my dress, though I can't imagine what sort of trouble a piece of jewelry might ward off. It's the thought that counts, right? I thank her with a hug.

"Back before midnight!" she calls to Ryan through the open door. "Nothing wholesome happens after that."

Colin opens the sliding van door for us and offers his hand to Mia as she steps up to get in. Surprisingly, she takes it and gives him a smile.

"Progress," Terra whispers to me as we follow her in.

The ride to the French Quarter is lively, with everyone talking and laughing. We all need a break from the tension of dealing with Eva and Madame DéSolé. It's good to forget our troubles, if only for a few hours.

We park near St. Peter Street to join Ryan's cousins on the parade route and are immediately engulfed in a sea of costumes. There are traditional vampires and devils, French sailors, and too many pirates to count. But the most beautiful costumes are worn by the men and women playing newlyweds with their faces elaborately painted as sugar skulls. Dresses of all colors, white and black, blood red and purple, and yards of lace swirl around us. The grooms dance with their walking sticks while the brides twirl parasols over their heads.

Ryan introduces us to his cousins, but the noise is so loud, we can only smile and wave at each other. A brass band leads the parade, playing "Iko Iko," and we all join the river of people flowing through the streets toward Jackson Square.

Crowds of costumed partiers throw Mardi Gras beads from the balconies above. Ryan and Colin catch handfuls of beads effortlessly and I see Colin place several strands around Mia's neck. *Progress indeed*, I think with a smile.

The energy and the music are intoxicating, and the night air is thick with the magic of it all. We pass a group of young men tap-dancing with bottle tops pressed into the soles of their shoes as people throw coins and dollars into a black hat on the ground in front of them.

We follow the parade until we get close to Bourbon Street, then break away and join the throngs there. Ryan's told me the parade never takes Bourbon Street, where a nonstop stream of foot traffic and revelers stretches as far as the eye can see.

As much as I enjoy it all, I notice Ryan and Colin carefully scanning the crowd. Ryan sees me watching him and smiles, but goes right back to watching the people around us.

We pass a darkened courtyard, and Terra suddenly turns to it and stops. The crowd noise and music are so loud, I have to yell even though I'm standing right next to her. "What is it?"

Terra points to the courtyard. "Madame DéSolé," she shouts into my ear.

The hair on the back of my neck stands up as I look where she's pointing. A woman stands in the middle of the courtyard, surrounded by a handful of other figures in dark, cloaked costumes. Strings of purple lights hang above the courtyard, bathing the group in an eerie glow. Like the "newlyweds" in the parade, everyone in the group wears white face paint, with circles of black around their eyes and rows of vertical black lines across their mouths to look like the grin of a skull.

With one look at the tall, thin woman who stands at the center of the group, I know Terra's right: it's got to be DéSolé.

Her high, prominent cheekbones enhance the effect of the makeup. Her jet black hair, pulled back in a tight bun, is matched by a black dress that clings tightly to her body from her slender shoulders to her ankles. Neon purple chokers lie in a stack around her neck, all the way up to her sharp jawline.

Her eyes meet mine, and with a sickening grin, she blows me a kiss. I press my hand against the St. Michael medallion by my heart. My dress suddenly feels far too tight, making it hard to breathe.

The rest of our group is nowhere in sight. Terra grabs my wrist and pulls me deeper into the crowd.

Just as I'm ready to panic, I see Ryan pushing his way back to us. "Hey, you have to stay close to me," he yells. "You're too short for me to see in the crowd."

"It was Madame DéSolé," I shout back frantically. "We saw her in the courtyard we just passed."

"Where?" he asks, craning his neck to see over the revelers.

I point, but the courtyard is empty. "They were there just a second ago!"

Terra nods, letting him know I wasn't the only one who saw them. As the rest of our group rejoins us, Ryan leans in to Colin and yells something in his ear, but I can't hear it over the band's horns and the revelry of the crowd. Colin gives him a nod and disappears into the sea of people once again.

"Come on, we're going back to Jackson Square." Ryan takes my hand and directs Terra to walk in front of us, yelling back to Cheddar, "Keep Mia close and follow us. We'll take a side street."

In a matter of seconds, we're away from the crowd and walking along St. Ann Street back to Jackson Square. "Where did Colin go?" Mia asks, looking back over her shoulder as we walk.

"DéSolé is looking for him. He'll keep her occupied and away from us."

"Are you sure he'll be okay?"

Ryan regards Mia with a wry smile. "This is new. You worried about him?"

"Uh, *no*," Mia says, trying way too hard to keep the concern out of her voice. "I'm talking tactics here. Is splitting up the smartest idea?"

"Lay your fears to rest," Ryan assures her, seeing right through the front. "He's got plenty of tricks up his sleeve."

We reach Jackson Square and Cheddar convinces Mia and Terra to join him at Café du Monde.

"Does he ever get enough to eat?" Ryan asks.

"I don't think so, but he tries really *really* hard," I say, laughing.

Carriages line Decatur Street alongside the square, and Ryan points to a red carriage with a thoroughly bored-looking mule waiting for his next fare. "How about a Halloween night tour?" he asks. Without waiting for an answer, he pays the driver. "Step right up, miss," he says, offering me his hand.

The night is still warm and humid, and the brightest of the stars twinkle faintly through the glow of city lights.

"No commentary needed, my friend," Ryan says as he tips the driver an extra ten dollars. "I'll be happy to share the points of interest with the young lady."

We stick to the less crowded streets, where the *clop clop clop* of the mule's hooves echo against the building fronts. The driver rings a bell at each intersection to alert the more distracted partiers.

Lavish Halloween decorations cover each home and business, and friends and families gather on the balconies, laughing and enjoying the night. "It'll be like this all night and well into the morning," Ryan says admiringly. His love for the city shows in his eyes.

I look up to the sky. "Did you notice? It's not raining."

He looks up as if to confirm, then back at me. "No, it's not," he says gently.

Choosing to take control of the moment, I lean over and kiss him on the cheek.

"How forward of you, Miss Tempest," he says.

"Despite my attire, I'm quite the modern girl."

In mock astonishment, he asks, "What would your sisters say?"

"They'd say you were a sucker for letting a little rain get in your way last night."

He smiles and takes my hand as we make the final turn back to Jackson Square.

Café du Monde is crowded with hungry revelers as the carriage pulls up to let us out. Ryan exits first, taking my hand again. We easily spot Mia, her blue dress a standout against the other costumes. She and Terra sip coffee while Cheddar balances a full box of beignets on his lap next to his pumpkin mask. "That mask get in your way, boss?" Ryan asks.

"I'm on a mission, man," Cheddar replies, happily stuffing his mouth.

Ryan scans the café's walls for a clock. "We'd better get back to Rosamie's. She'll be a devil if I get you all back after midnight."

Mia stares into the Square, mesmerized by something only she can see. As we walk back to the van, she whispers to me that it was full of people dancing, their dresses similar in style to the vintage ones we have on. "It was beautiful."

"Is that romance in your voice?" I tease.

"It wasn't *me* dancing; just reporting what I saw," she says, twirling her ponytail.

"Oh, please," Terra chimes in from behind us. "I can

feel it on you. If Colin hadn't disappeared, I'm pretty sure it would have been you two in the carriage."

"The way he's been fawning over you, I can think of worse fates," I add.

Giving us her most powerful death glare, Mia walks swiftly ahead of us without another word.

Terra links her arm in mine and sighs, "*L'amour!* But alas, it's a pirate's life for me."

Back at the plantation, we enter Rosamie's house quietly. The children have come and gone, and the sugar candles have almost completely melted in their pumpkin shelters.

After changing back into our regular clothes, Cheddar and the twins head to the cottages and I walk Ryan to the van. "Thank you for a lovely evening," I say with another curtsy, which isn't half as dramatic in jeans and a sweatshirt.

Ryan loosens his tie and wraps the green satin around my neck. "A souvenir of your first Halloween in New Orleans."

"Thank you, sir."

"You're most welcome. I'll be back early tomorrow and we'll take a drive to Eva's. The sooner we resolve the business of the book, the better for everyone. DéSolé has been patient up until now, but that's not likely to last much longer."

Remembering our encounter with Madame DéSolé, I ask, "Why did she blow me a kiss?"

"She blew you a kiss?" Ryan looks puzzled for a moment, but quickly shrugs it off. "Just trying to rattle your cage, I'm sure. Like I said before, DéSolé's all smoke and mirrors. It's not that she isn't trouble, because she certainly is. But she likes to make people nervous. She thinks it strengthens her position."

"Well, it's working," I say with a shudder.

"Don't let it get to you. I know how strong you are, especially around your sisters. DéSolé's got nothing the three of you can't handle."

In this moment, I know he's right. As unsettling as it was, I refuse to let my fear get the better of me. If we can get the book back tomorrow and return it to Colin, there will be little reason for her to stay interested in us.

We look up again to the night sky. The stars are brighter here on the plantation, away from the lights of the city. A moment later, they're blocked out by Ryan's face as he kisses me, gently, on the lips.

It only lasts a second or three, but my cheeks blaze as he breaks the kiss and goes back to looking up at the sky. "I'm no sucker. Tell your sisters that timing is everything."

"Duly noted," I reply, unable to keep from smiling.

"Tomorrow's the Day of the Dead," he says as he gets into the van and turns the ignition. "Before we meet Eva, we'll go to the cemetery and visit my mom."

"That sounds—" I'm about to say *amazing*, but catch myself because that would sound horrible, though no better adjectives spring to mind. "—lovely, I guess?"

He smiles, putting the van in gear. "I know what you mean. See you in the morning."

As he rolls off across the crunching gravel, I circle to

the back of the house and continue along the pathway to the guest cottages. But I haven't made it halfway before a faint glow catches my eye from just beyond the fence. I stop in my tracks, straining my eyes into the gloom. The glow is neon purple—the same color as DéSolé's necklaces were in that darkened courtyard in the French Quarter.

My breath catches in my throat. I remind myself of what Ryan said: DéSolé is just trying to rattle me. I remember that she can't step on the property, and I've still got the St. Michael medal that Rosamie gave me in my hip pocket.

Yet, I can't move. I stand frozen with terror in the middle of the path. I'm not entirely sure my heart's even beating.

Something brushes against my pant leg and I jump about a foot, barely managing to bite back a scream. Looking down, I see it's just Miracle. "You scared me to death," I scold, certain she can understand me. *On the other hand*, I tell myself, *at least I'm sure my heart's beating.*

Miracle rubs against my legs, walking a circle around me, then takes a few steps toward the cottages and stops. She looks out into the darkness and hisses.

"My thoughts exactly," I say as I watch the purple neon fade.

Miracle walks back to me and stands on her hind legs, pawing at me to pick her up. I take her in my arms and cradle her against my chest, where her low, continuous purr calms my heart. "You've been taking lessons from Terra," I say, stroking her fur as we walk to the cottage.

Once inside, I close and lock the door as Miracle jumps onto Mia's bed. "Of course," I whisper, watching her burrow behind Mia's legs. I lean over the bed, petting her one last time for the night. "Do me a favor, Miracle—sleep with one eye open."

CHAPTER
7

OCTOBER SLIPS AWAY and November quietly takes its place during the peaceful night. Miracle never stirred, but I'd like to think if we'd been in danger, she would have defended us. I scratch her behind the ears before getting dressed. The twins, still fast asleep, take no notice as I slip out the door to meet Ryan.

As I walk along the path to the front of the house, mist rises from the earth, warmed by a just-rising sun. The lush landscape gives no indication that fall is in full swing. It doesn't seem possible that Thanksgiving is just three weeks away.

Ryan waits for me on the front steps of the house with two large coffees.

"You're really trying to get on my good side, aren't you?" I ask, taking one.

"Thought I already was," he says as he leans in and kisses my cheek.

"Keep bringing me coffee and you'll stay there. What happened last night with Colin and Madame DéSolé?"

"I have no idea. He didn't come home."

"That's normal, though, right?" I ask.

"For the most part. But we were supposed to meet back up after I dropped you off."

"Are you worried?"

"Not just yet, but we'll see what the day brings," he says as he stands and takes my hand. "Let's hit the road before the rest of your crew wakes up."

Before heading to Eva's to retrieve the book, we stop at Saint Louis Cemetery to visit the tomb of Ryan's and Colin's mother and place flowers that Rosamie gathered just after sunrise.

Gray and white stone vaults stand above ground in rows and aisles that seem to go on forever. Small groups of people are gathered, placing brightly colored flowers and candles to honor their departed family members. We wander the cemetery, admiring the vases of orange and yellow marigolds and the jewel-hued candle holders as Ryan points out the tombs of other relatives who have come to this place for their final rest.

We finally reach the vault we've come to tend, surrounded by gray cement brick, the front sealed in ivory marble. An alabaster angel lies atop, weeping silently with her face buried in one arm as the other hangs gracefully over the side of the vault. Ryan and Colin have kept the monument tidy since they were old enough to join their grandmother on her weekly visits. Delicately carved roses and vines frame the name, CORDELIA GRACE BROUSSARD, followed by her date of birth and date of death—Ryan and Colin's birthday.

Ryan kneels and makes the sign of the cross before pressing his fingers to his lips and touching the marble just above her name. I stand back, allowing him time and space to offer his silent prayer. When he stands, he hands me half of the flowers to lay at the base of the tomb.

"My grandmother said she was kind, and laughed easily," he says with a faraway smile, gazing at the treetops as they shudder and sway in the breeze. "She was always singing."

"She sounds amazing," I say, gently arranging white and pale-peach roses.

"She would have loved you." Ryan pulls several candleholders from the basket Rosamie left for us and places votive candles in each, lighting them with long wooden matches. "Candles to renew the light we lost when you left us, Mom," he murmurs.

"I wish she could have seen you grow up," I say, taking his hand.

"Me too," he sighs. "More for Colin's sake than mine. He might not have gotten so lost."

I feel his pain as sharply as if it were my own. For him and his brother, the promise of a loving family was broken before it had a chance to be kept.

I try to imagine what Colin would have been like if their lives had taken a different course. Would he have worried about Ryan and watched out for him, instead of the other way around? Would their bond have been stronger without the blame that Colin placed on his brother?

As if reading my thoughts, Ryan answers, "Life had different plans for us all." He places his hand once more on the roof of the tomb and gives it a final kiss. It's beyond unfair that he'll never place a kiss on her cheek. "Well," he says, coming back to the here and now, "on to the next. Let's go visit your mother and see about getting that book back."

Although we have to go, part of me wishes we could stay in the serenity of the cemetery and pretend we have nothing to do for the rest of the day.

As we leave the cemetery and walk toward the French Quarter, I try to quiet the voice in my head that wonders what will happen when we get to Eva's.

We reach the St. Philip, and a woman with impossibly blue eyes and long, colorful dreadlocks calls out to Ryan from in front of the gated entryway. "Ryan Laurent! Where have you been hiding yourself?"

"Tyler! Looking gorgeous as always." Ryan hugs her, planting a kiss on her cheek, and then gestures to me. "Tyler, this is Emerald. She came to enjoy Halloween in our beautiful city."

She gives me a brilliant smile. "If you're a friend of Ryan's, you're good people. I trust you had fun last night?"

"I did," I say, letting her squeeze my hand warmly in both of hers. "It's incredible here."

"That it is. People come to visit and never leave. Like me," she laughs as she opens the wrought-iron gate to welcome us into the elaborately decorated courtyard. A scrappy trio of Chihuahuas bark at us as we walk through. "Don't mind them," Tyler says, securing the gate behind us. "They're just saying hello."

"We're here to see Eva Tempest," Ryan says. "Emerald is her daughter."

"Really?" Tyler tilts her head to one side, appraising me with a closer eye. "I didn't know Eva had a daughter."

"It was news to us too," I say. "She's actually got three."

Without missing a beat, she replies, "Well, that *is* some news. You go on up. If I don't take these dogs for a walk, we'll never hear the end of it. Eva's in Apartment 7."

We climb the darkened stairs to the second floor. A red door with a brass "7" greets us at the second landing. Ryan gives me a reassuring look as I knock quietly on the door. Getting no answer for maybe half a minute—though it might as well be an hour—I knock again.

Nothing.

I turn the handle and crack the door open a few inches. "Eva? It's Em and Ryan," I call as I open the door further. The apartment is silent as we step inside.

There are only two rooms, the first containing a bed and writing desk. A short hallway connects to a smaller room with French doors that open onto a balcony facing the street. An old air conditioner tries unsuccessfully to cool the oppressive heat. Blood-red drapes keep out the worst of the midday glare, but make it hard to see much else in the dim room until our eyes adjust.

On the floor in the corner of the smaller room, Eva sits completely still in the semidarkness.

Ryan stays near the apartment door as I move

tentatively up the hallway and kneel beside her. "Eva, what are you doing?"

She doesn't acknowledge me until I brush a lock of hair out of her face so I can look in her eyes. Tears tumble down her cheeks as she looks at me. "I wanted to go back. I wanted to make it right."

"I know, Mom," I say, struggling now to hold back my own tears.

"You girls were precious and innocent—the only good thing I've ever done in this life." She drops her head into her hands as her shoulders begin shaking.

"Mom, don't cry," I say, stroking her hair.

"I'm so sorry, Emerald. I wasn't ready. I was a child myself. After all these years, and all my failures, I don't think I ever would have been ready. I left you with my mother because it was the best thing I could do for the three of you—to keep you safe from *me*," she sobs.

I move completely down to the floor, tucking my legs to the side, and wrap my arms around her, pulling her in tight. Feeling her sobbing in my arms, the last of my resolve dissipates and we cry together, rocking back and forth. I feel like a lost child who's been brought home, the last broken pieces of my heart beginning to mend themselves as Eva releases all of her pain and regret into the safe place between us.

I take another deep breath and slow time down, allowing us to allay years of deceit and regret while soothing her heart. We continue to rock in the shadows of the room until our tears begin to subside.

"Mom," I say as I pull away just enough to look into

her eyes, "I love you. We'll find our way through this, in time. I happen to have plenty of it, in case you forgot."

She smiles sadly. "Can I even hope Mia's heart is as forgiving as yours?"

"More than you might realize," I say, thinking of how Mia seems to have softened toward Colin in the past day or two. "But you need to talk with her. You need to give her a *chance* to forgive you."

She looks up at me, a world of pain in her eyes. "I don't know how."

"Neither does she, Mom. But we'll figure it out together."

She reaches out to me, and in that moment, I feel like a parent comforting a heartbroken child. I accept her remorse and vulnerability and tuck it all into my heart, giving her a place to fall, wrapped safely in my arms.

After a few minutes more, I help her to her feet and lead her to the bathroom. Carefully brushing her hair, I pull it back into a long ponytail and soak a washcloth with cool water to wipe the tears from her face. "Good as new," I say as we both look into the mirror. I see her face in mine, and mine in hers.

Although her eyes are still red and puffy, a faint smile crosses her face. "You're a beautiful, brave girl," she says.

"So are you." I give her a kiss on the cheek and lead her back out to the main room.

Ryan stands quietly by the door, doing his best to allow us our space. I sit Eva on the edge of her bed, getting her a glass of water before asking her gently, "Eva—where's the book?"

She gulps the water down and sets the glass carefully on her nightstand. She looks to me, then stands and walks to the closet. She opens the slender door slowly, then looks to Ryan. "Would you please reach up to the top shelf? There's a box pushed to the very back, under a blanket."

Ryan joins her at the closet and reaches up, easily finding the box. He hands it to her with a reassuring smile. In that moment, I realize how much it means to have him here. I know I could've handled this alone, but his self-assured presence has given the situation a calmness and sense of safety.

Eva sits back down on the bed, placing the box on her lap. She runs her hands over the top and sides of the box, closing her eyes. Breathing in deeply, she holds the air in her lungs for a moment, then slowly exhales. "I wanted things to be different, to make everything right again. But I know now that the solutions aren't in this book. They never were." Holding the book in both hands, she offers it to me.

"Thank you, Mom," I say, taking it. "We'll find the solutions together. You, me, and the girls."

She nods slightly, then smiles. "A new start, then?"

"A new start," I say, smiling back.

We leave Eva to freshen up before she goes to work, shutting the door quietly behind us. We walk down the stairs, out to the sidewalk and into the sunlight, leaving the darkness behind.

Tyler and her Chihuahuas are returning from their walk as passersby shout their hellos. She laughs and waves.

"This city loves you, Tyler," says Ryan.

"The feeling is entirely mutual, love."

"Can you do me a favor?" he asks.

"Sure, anything," she says, trying to untangle the leashes while the dogs run around Ryan's legs.

"Keep an eye on Eva? Things are, well, a little weird."

Tyler looks at me reassuringly, her bright blue eyes full of kindness and compassion. "Of course. And, when aren't they around here?" she adds, winking as she turns to step through the gate and close up. She waves goodbye as the dogs bounce happily, taking treats Tyler pulls from a pouch around her waist.

As we walk, Ryan puts his arm around my shoulder.

"Thank you," I say, without elaborating, as he pulls me closer.

"She's going to be okay," he says. "We all will."

His certainty reassures me. After seeing Eva at her weakest moment, I want to believe that our family can move forward together. Even Mia.

We stop at a small café to grab a bite to eat. While we wait in line to order our food, Ryan calls Rosamie to see if she's heard from Colin. As he listens, he rolls his eyes and I can tell we're not staying to eat. "We need to get back to the plantation," he says after disconnecting.

He pulls me out of line, leaving the delicious smell of frying chicken behind. I struggle to keep up, his long strides outpacing my own as we make our way back to the van.

His face is impossible to read as he drives, but I can tell he's struggling to keep within the speed limits.

When we pull up to Rosamie's front steps, Mia and Terra await us on the porch. I jump out of the van, holding the book over my head in triumph, but before I can get a word out, Mia rushes down the steps.

"We need to find Colin," she says with an urgency in her tone that alarms me.

"What have you heard?" Ryan asks.

"It's just a feeling," Mia says, looking away. She knows more than she's saying. Since sharing the secret of my charm with Ryan, I'm hoping he doesn't press her for more information and just takes her at her word.

For a moment, it doesn't look like he will. He gives her a probing look, but nods once. "All right. I'm going inside to check with Rose. We'll leave in a few minutes."

I hand him the book. "Give this to Rose for safekeeping." In Rosamie's care, it'll be safe until we find Colin and decide our next move.

Mia looks relieved as Ryan bounds up the steps and into the house. Once he's inside, she turns to us. "Wyatt doesn't know where Colin is. He thinks Madame DéSolé is using some kind of trick to keep him hidden. She's trying to draw us out."

"As long as we stay together, we'll be safe," Terra says, answering my question before I ask it.

Ryan, Cheddar, and Rosamie come out to join us and Rosamie pulls me aside. "Do you still have the St. Michael pendant I gave you?"

I nod, clutching the snakeskin pouch in my pocket.

"Keep it with you at all times. And don't lose sight of each other," she warns.

We leave her in front of the house, waving after us as our van rumbles down the gravel drive.

"Do you have a 'feeling' about where we should look?" Ryan asks, glancing at Mia in the rearview.

"We should start at the swamp," she says, staring out the window as the landscape rushes past us. "Near the place we had lunch."

Ryan glances at me. I nod. Without telling him how Mia knows, I can only reassure him it's the right plan of action.

"There's an old fishing cabin maybe a quarter-mile from that spot," he says. "We used to spend the night there when we were younger."

We reach the entrance to the swamp and Ryan rents a boat large enough to carry us all. Heavy clouds diffuse the afternoon light, and a gentle, warm rain begins to fall as Ryan starts the boat's engine. Cruising slowly along the waterways, the rain and mist give the trees a ghostly appearance. Spanish moss, heavy with water, sways as the gusts grow in intensity. Not exactly the ideal conditions to be out searching for someone, but we have little choice.

At last we come to a narrow, rickety dock leading up to a log cabin that's definitely seen better days. The windows are all smashed out, only a few pieces of jagged dirty glass remaining, and what looks like poison ivy snakes in and around the windows and front door. "How long has it been since you guys stayed here?" asks Cheddar.

"Not since grade school," Ryan answers as he hitches the boat to a wooden post.

We walk up the dock to the cabin, the towering cypress trees all around us creaking and groaning like ghosts in the wind. Mia tries to gather her wildly swirling hair into a ponytail. "I knew I should have brought more clothes," she says, directly to me.

"It's not like you had rain gear at home, Mia," I say, helping her secure her hair. The tennis shoes and sweatshirts we're in will have to do, but we'll be soaked through before long.

The sinking sun filters through swaying treetops, and dapples of light and shade make the cabin's façade look almost like a living face grimacing at us. The front door stands ajar, and as Ryan approaches it, something cries out—almost a gurgling scream—from the canopy of trees above, nearly making me jump out of my skin.

"Just an egret," Ryan tells us over his shoulder. Looking around at Cheddar and the girls' colorless faces, I take comfort in knowing I'm not the only one who needed the reassurance.

Ryan passes through the door and the rest of us follow him inside.

Rusty fishing gear rests forgotten on the room's one table, and empty food cans litter the floor. In frustration, Ryan kicks a can to one corner of the room. "No one's been here for a long time."

"We need to look around the land surrounding this place," Mia says.

Ryan eyes her again and I can tell he's about to ask

her where this is coming from. He doesn't know what I, and no doubt Terra, have long since realized: that Wyatt is in the cabin with us, giving Mia direction.

I step over to Ryan. "Please," I say. "She knows what she's talking about."

He lets out a deep breath. "Okay. But it'll be dark soon and if we don't find anything, we'll have to give it up until tomorrow."

We leave the cabin and make our way around to the land behind it. "I'll lead," says Ryan. "Girls stay in the middle and, Cheddar, you bring up the rear. Mia, I don't know why I'm agreeing to this, but… tell me where to go. Just don't direct us into any quicksand."

We walk, single file, through a network of barely visible trails. Ryan pushes overgrown vines and tree branches out of our way as we go, Mia telling him periodically when we need to change direction.

"We're being watched," Terra tells us, quiet enough for Ryan and Cheddar not to hear. "I can't see them, but I can feel it."

"It's DéSolé's people, but Colin isn't with them," Mia whispers back, clearly relaying the information from Wyatt.

The rain falls harder as we go deeper into the woods, the ground growing wetter and muddier with each step. We're all soaked, and the light's fading fast, but none of us wants to leave without finding Colin.

"We can only go so much farther," Ryan calls back to us over the sound of the wind and rain. "We'll give it five more minutes before we have to turn back."

As we walk further, fighting the mud, and with dense plant life obscuring most of our view in all directions, Terra grabs my arm. "Something isn't right. We shouldn't keep going this way."

I can barely hear her over the storm. "What do you mean?" I yell, wiping rain out of my eyes.

"We shouldn't go any farther," she shouts back.

"We'll turn around in five minutes." I'm so busy fumbling through the reeds that I bump into Ryan, who's stopped in his tracks.

"Hold on," he calls back to the others.

We stand at a break in the reeds, and the trail opens up ahead of us. Less than twenty feet away stand three figures dressed in white. I can't make out their faces in the darkness and heavy rain, but they look like men.

"Who are you?" Ryan calls.

The figures say nothing, standing completely motionless.

Ryan turns to me. "Go back the other way."

Just as we turn around, Mia yells, "*Run!*"

Ryan takes my hand and we break into as fast a run as we can manage in an overgrown bog. "Cheddar, stay close behind the girls," he yells as we stumble through the plants and mud, trying to find our way in the almost pitch black.

I look back every few feet, trying to see if the men are following us, but I can't make out anything beyond Cheddar until, to my relief, I can see the faint silhouette of the cabin ahead. "We're almost there!"

We round the cabin and make our way down the

dock as fast as we can. As soon as we reach the boat, I turn around to help the twins get in. But when I do, my heart drops.

Cheddar is nowhere in sight.

CHAPTER
8

STANDING IN THE DARKNESS AND RAIN, in the chaos of the blowing wind, it takes me a few seconds to process that Cheddar's gone. The realization feels like a punch in the stomach as I look back up the dock.

He isn't coming.

I start to run back for him, but Ryan stops me. "We have to go back," I scream, "we can't leave him there!" Raindrops and tears run down my cheeks.

"Em, we have to get out of here," Ryan yells back, pulling me toward the boat. "If we don't, we'll be stuck."

"We *can't!*" I plead.

Mia and Terra take my arms. "It'll be okay, we'll find him," Terra yells.

I try to push them away, but exhaustion overtakes me.

"We have to go, Em," Mia says, shaking me. "Wyatt will help us find him, but we have to leave now."

I look back at the cabin, despair preventing me from fighting any more.

Ryan starts the boat and pushes the throttle forward as we speed away from the dock. I watch as the cabin disappears behind us, the deep purples and blacks of night swallowing up everything in view.

By the time we get back to the van, we're completely soaked and shivering. Silent tears continue as I step up into the passenger seat and Mia and Terra huddle together behind me.

Ryan says nothing as he pulls out of the parking lot, driving us back to the plantation.

Everything feels wrong, like I've lost control. Earlier today I was so sure that we'd get the book back, that Eva and Mia would start the work of mending their relationship, and that we'd make things right again.

Now it's all shattered. My thoughts race but there's no solution. I can't fix it. I can only sit here in silence, watching the rain hit the windshield. The wipers move rapidly back and forth, the road ahead of us barely visible.

When we arrive at the plantation, the lights in Rosamie's windows offer some comfort. I have no words for Ryan as I get out of the van. I slam the door behind me and the twins help me up the front steps.

The van idles for a moment, then pulls away, back into the storm.

Rose meets us at the door and pulls me inside first. "What in heaven's name happened?" she asks, surveying us as we stand, dripping wet, in her entryway. "Where are the boys?"

"We couldn't find Colin, and now Cheddar's missing," I manage to say before bursting into fresh tears.

"Oh, now, it's all right," she says calmly. "You're in the worst shape; I'll run a hot bath for you. Mia, Terra, get fresh clothes from the cottage and come right back."

As the twins fetch our clothing, Rose leads me to the master bathroom. She turns the water on full force with steaming hot water and pours lavender-scented oil under the tap. She wraps a thick towel around me before lighting sugar candles around the tub.

Before leaving me, she takes me by the shoulders and looks me in the eyes. "You listen to me. Colin knows his way around the swamp. And Cheddar is a strong boy; he's going to find his way back to you all," she says fiercely.

All I can do is nod and tremble, the cold seeping into my bones.

"There are fresh towels next to the tub. You get those wet clothes off and stay in that tub until you are completely thawed out. I'll send your sisters up with warm clothes for you." She hugs me tightly before leaving, closing the bathroom door as she goes.

I turn to see my reflection in the vanity mirror. My hair hangs in wet strands, and splatters of mud cover my face and clothes. This same time last night, I was in a beautiful dress, celebrating Halloween. Now, I'm looking at a girl I don't recognize.

I peel off my clothes and leave them in a muddy pile

on the floor. Steam rises from the tub as I step in, taking in a deep breath of lavender as I lie back. I relax into the heat and comfort of the water, and close my eyes.

I try to keep from crying as I think of Cheddar, still in the swamp, cold, wet, and alone. It's no use and I lie there for a long time, quiet sobs making ripples in the bathwater.

Eventually, the tears subside and I open my eyes. The candlelight casts a warm glow against pale-lavender walls. Stacks of thick white towels tied with purple ribbon sit on a small table next to the tub, and a glossy black soap dish holds lavender soap on the vanity. I admire the calming beauty of it until I see my muddy clothing sitting in a puddle of brown water on the otherwise perfectly clean, black-and-white floor tile.

"Ugh," I sigh.

I wash my hair and drain the tub. As I watch the soapy water swirl down the drain, I feel a deep pang of homesickness.

I miss Mama, her warm hugs, and her home-cooked meals. I miss the library with its little fireplace, and the refuge of its book-lined shelves. I want to find Cheddar and go home to sit on our beach while the ebb and flow of the surf lends order to my thoughts and makes everything clear again. I want to leave Eva and the book here, and get back to a place that isn't wrapped in mystery and confusion. And I want to leave the Laurent brothers behind.

I don't blame Ryan for what happened in the swamp, but my feelings for him have clouded my judgment. I let myself fall into a false sense of security, as though he could keep us all from harm. The only people I trust completely are my sisters, and I want to get back to trusting myself.

As I dry myself off and wrap my hair in a towel, there's a soft knock at the door. "It's Mia." She comes in before I can answer and hands me my clothes, shutting the door behind her. "Nice bathroom, but you know you're cleaning up that pile of muddy clothes, right?" she says, trying to get me to laugh.

All I manage is a halfhearted smile as I button my jeans.

"It's going to be okay," she says, her tone softening. "We'll find him."

"We shouldn't have left him behind," I say quietly, pulling my sweatshirt over my head.

"What good would we have been to him if we'd stayed there, Em?" she asks as she picks up a brush and works the tangles out of my hair. "If we'd gotten caught in a flood—or worse, caught by DéSolé's people?"

"Cheddar wouldn't have left any of us there," I reply.

Her eyes meet mine in the glass of the mirror. She sets the brush down and turns toward me, wrapping me in a hug.

Terra slips into the room behind us, forgoing the knock entirely. "Rosamie has hot tea and soup downstairs, next to the fireplace. Ew, you know you're cleaning up those muddy clothes, right?"

I'm able to manage a laugh this time.

We gather the wet towels and clothes and make our

way back downstairs to the warmth of the fireplace. Miracle lies curled up beside a roaring fire, and Rosamie's made up beds for us on the couches and floor.

"I think it's best if you three stay in here tonight," Rose says with a warm smile that immediately makes me feel better. "Your guardian isn't likely to move from her spot, so you might as well join her." We sit cross-legged on the floor, quietly eating chicken soup with fluffy dumplings and washing it down with chamomile tea. I don't have much of an appetite, imagining Cheddar out in the elements and undoubtedly hungry.

The cold and damp have finally left my body and my eyes begin to close, heavy with exhaustion. "Get some sleep, and don't waste a minute of it on worry," Rose says as she collects our dishes. "Cheddar will be back, eating me out of house and home, in no time at all."

She dims the lights and leaves as Miracle proves her wrong, rising from her cushion to curl up behind Mia's knees.

Lying on the couch with only the light from the fire, I feel a wave of guilt wash over me. Cheddar has been there for my family through thick and thin. He'd do anything for us. Thinking of him lost in the swamp, I realize we should have told him about our charms before we came to New Orleans, if not years earlier. It feels like a betrayal to have kept it from him. Maybe it would be a comfort to him, wherever he is now. I have to believe that he'll be okay, that we'll find him. And when we do, we'll tell him everything.

I fall asleep watching the flames dance and cast

shadows across the living room, and wake in the morning to the smell of coffee and bright sun in my eyes.

The twins are in the dining room chatting with Rosamie and I join them at the table after pouring a cup of coffee. "Well!" says Rose. "You don't look much more rested than when you went to sleep last night."

I shrug my shoulders, staring into my coffee as I stir in the sugar and a swirling splash of cream. "I didn't sleep much. At least, it doesn't feel like I did." In fact, I tossed and turned most of the night away, dreaming things I only remember as shadowy and frightening.

"You slept fine," Terra says. "But your snoring kept Mia and me awake. I think you have swamp water in your sinuses."

I start to laugh, then catch myself, thinking of Cheddar.

"Em, stop feeling guilty," Mia says softly.

"How can I? We're here and Cheddar isn't."

"If we had stayed behind, there's a chance we'd *all* be missing right now. Now we can regroup and go back to find him. And we *will* find him, Em." Mia says it emphatically, perhaps trying to convince herself more than me.

"He's a strong one, and he's got a fierce love for you girls," Rosamie says. "That kind of loyalty will keep a man from falling victim to a wide array of evils. You'd do well not to count him out."

"We'll find him," says Terra. "He's too big to go missing for long."

I look up from my coffee, and Terra's eyes are warm

and soothing. I know she's sending me reassuring vibrations.

Just as I'm starting to relax, a pounding comes at the front door and we all jump up at once, following Rose to the foyer. She swings the door open to Ryan and Colin holding up a semiconscious Cheddar, covered in mud, between them. "Hurry, bring him inside," Rose commands. "Emerald, wet some towels with hot water and meet us in the living room."

Ryan and Colin carry Cheddar into the house and lay him carefully on the couch. Rosamie tells them to undress him and cover him with a quilt and orders Mia and Terra to get a warm change of clothes from the guest cottage.

Rose joins me in the kitchen to brew peppermint tea and heat up soup from the night before. "We need to get him cleaned up, and then try to get the tea and soup in him as quick as possible. He must be warmed and hydrated immediately."

She works with the speed and precision of a field doctor, ordering everyone about and making fast work of getting the mud off of Cheddar, and the tea and soup into him. He becomes alert long enough to take a few sips, but is out cold within moments.

Ryan builds another fire and lays a new stack of wood next to the fireplace just before Rose orders all of us out of the living room so Cheddar can rest. "I'll stay here with him," she says as she closes the room's double doors. "You five go make peace with each other."

In awkward silence, we step outside to the front

porch. Mia's the first to speak, immediately taking aim at Colin: "Where were you, and what happened to Cheddar?"

Colin huffs, then spits over the side of the porch. "It's none of your business where I was. But I found him with DéSolé Marchand. She planned on keeping him until you three gave the book back."

"What did they do to him?" Mia asks, her voice rising in volume.

"He was struggling and she blew conjure powder in his face," Colin explains.

"It's just one of DéSolé's tricks," Ryan says. "He'll be in and out of sleep for a few days, but he'll be okay."

"Oh, that's all?" Mia shrills, her anger just barely under control.

"This isn't my fault, Mia," Colin says, his composure beginning to crack. "I was trying to protect you, to buy you time until you got the book back from your mother."

"It's *completely* your fault," she yells. "None of this would have happened if you hadn't come to Santa Cruz looking for that stupid book. Which, by the way, can't help you at all!"

"What do you mean?" Colin says, his calm rapidly faltering.

"Wyatt is dead," Mia says, cutting through all pretense.

For a moment, Colin looks as though Mia's just slapped him, hard and out of nowhere. He glares at her, shaking his head from side to side. "That's not true. You don't know anything about it."

"I know all about it," she says.

"Mia, don't," I say, trying to keep her from saying anything she—all of us—might regret.

"No! This has gone far enough," she says defiantly. She take a few steps toward Colin and pauses. I have the sickening feeling that she's taking direction from Wyatt and that all of our secrets are about to get spilled all over Rosamie's porch. "I'll prove it to you. Ask me something only Wyatt would know," she challenges.

"That's ridiculous," Colin replies, sitting down in one of the porch chairs and crossing his arms.

Ryan speaks up. "Ask her, Colin."

Colin stares at his brother for a moment, first in confusion, then with a look of fear in his eyes that he tries to mask with anger. "Either you don't know what you're talking about, or you're messing with me," he bites off ferociously. "I don't recommend messing with me. Not about that."

His menacing posture and the way his nostrils flare remind me of the way he looked the day we stood face to face in our front entryway in Santa Cruz—the first time he confronted me in search of that stupid book. But I was too terrified, then, to see the fear beneath his vicious exterior. It was there in his eyes all along, I'm sure, but I didn't know him then; didn't know what a deeply frightened person he really was.

"Colin," Ryan says pleadingly, placing a hand on his brother's shoulder, "just ask her."

Colin looks at Mia, then slowly asks his question. "What was the last thing Wyatt said to me?"

Mia pauses, listening to an answer only she can hear. Then, unable to make eye contact with Colin, she looks down at her feet. "He said, 'If this plan to go back in time works, try and grow up to be less of a jerk next time.' "

Colin stares at her. It pains me to watch the menace and the anger slip away only to be replaced by dawning horror and grief.

He practically collapses into one of the porch chairs, hiding his face in his hands as he begins to weep.

"The only way you can help Wyatt now is to accept that he's gone," Mia tells him. It's the most gently I've ever heard her speak to Colin. "If you don't, you're keeping him trapped in between worlds. He can't move freely—he's tied to you."

"No, no, no," is all Colin can say.

Ryan bends down, presses his head to Colin's, and holds him as he cries.

After a few moments, Terra sits in the chair next to Colin's and squeezes his shoulder, closing her eyes. I watch as she generates the most loving, healing vibration she can, pushing it through Colin and into Ryan so that both are held in its serene power.

As Colin's tears subside, Ryan stands and reaches out to Terra, pulling her into a tight hug.

On some level, he understands what she's done.

He releases Terra and turns to me, his eyes red and tired and his shoulders slouched with exhaustion.

"Terra, go inside and sit with Cheddar," I say as Mia takes Terra's place next to Colin. "Come with me," I tell Ryan, taking his hand to lead him down the front steps and onto the path, back to the bench where we sat under the stars what seems like a lifetime ago.

He sits, resting his head in his hands as I tell him everything I know to be true about the charms my sisters and I possess and what he's just experienced. I explain Mia's ability to talk to people across dimensions, Terra's ability to control and create vibrations, and even the night we merged, combining our powers, back in Santa Cruz.

He sits quietly for several moments, no questions asked, staring out at the land and trees.

"I don't understand it all, Ryan," I say, breaking the silence. "I just know that we've grown up this way. It's who we are."

"If you had told me all of this when I first met you, I wouldn't have believed it," he says, turning to face me. "With everything that's happened, though, I can't think of a better explanation. But now it's too dangerous here. You and your sisters have to go back to Santa Cruz."

"Absolutely not," I say. "We came here to find Eva, and to get the book back into the hands of your family. And now we have to confront DéSolé."

"Em, I can't protect you."

"I don't need your protection," I reply flatly. "I'm not running away from this."

"Everyone I care about is at risk," he says as Rosamie walks up the path toward us.

"Looks like I'm interrupting a very serious conversation," she says.

"Rose, you have to convince Emerald to take Mia

and Terra back to Santa Cruz," Ryan says. "It's not safe for them here."

"Cheddar's condition is proof positive of that," she replies by way of agreement. "But the girls are here for a reason. You need to let them finish what they came to do."

"I couldn't keep Cheddar safe—how am I supposed to protect them?" he asks defensively.

"Have you considered that perhaps it's not your job to protect them? They've managed to survive for years without your help. Together, they're stronger than me, you, Colin, and DéSolé put together."

"Is that so?" Ryan asks, trying not to smile.

"It is. Now you make yourself useful and tend to your brother. He needs you more than this young woman here ever will." Her words convince me, even if Ryan's still on the fence. As he leaves, Rose takes his place on the bench and takes my hand. "Emerald, you're the one to do this. You know that, right?"

"I do," I say.

"DéSolé Marchand is a strong woman, but her strength lies in her ability to confuse people with lies, making them question themselves. It's how she got to Colin so quickly. He's been lost since their mother died. DéSolé took that pain and twisted it to control him. But she can't work that same power over you and your sisters. Never forget that."

"What's going to happen to Colin?" I ask.

"He's going to work through things on his own time. He carries darkness with him like a coat of armor. He's looking for answers that don't exist and it's caught him in a downward spiral. But since you girls arrived, I've seen a change in him. His feelings for Mia have put a crack in that armor and there's still a chance he can get back on the right path."

Miracle jumps up into Rose's lap, pawing at her for attention. "Oh, you old black cat, what have you been up to?" she says as she strokes Miracle's back, where the fur shines blue-black in the sun.

"For now, you girls need a reality check," Rosamie goes on. "I'll have Ryan and Colin take you down to the Lower Ninth Ward to see what real pain looks like. There's nothing like seeing someone else's problems to make yours seem not so bad. It's still a mess down there, even after all these years. Hurricane Katrina changed the course of countless lives, and battered more than the city." She gently places her hand just over her heart.

Miracle jumps down and walks the path back toward the house, stopping a few steps ahead to make sure we're following.

Mia and Colin are still on the porch and his smile gives me hope that Mia's helped him turn a corner. Miracle ascends the stairs and rubs up against Mia's legs, purring. "Looks like you've got two admirers, Mia," says Rose, winking. "Colin, you and your brother are to take the girls into the Lower Ninth for the day. I'll tend to Cheddar; he'll need a couple of days to recover."

"You gonna be all right here without us?" Colin asks jokingly as he stands up, towering over all of us.

"Please," Rosamie laughs. "You know better than

to even ask. Now, come in and grab some water for the road."

Miracle follows Colin and Rose into the house as I hug Mia. "You okay?"

She nods. "Will be. Colin, too. I told him everything. I think he's finally starting to understand that what happened to Wyatt wasn't his fault."

"How did he take hearing about our charms?" I ask.

She laughs. "He said he always thought we were weird, and now he knows why. He did ask if I could talk to his mother for him, but I told him she's never come to me."

For a moment, I wonder why Ryan and Colin's mother hasn't come to Mia. But the ability to control time doesn't give me all the answers. I wish it did.

"Colin wants to help us finish this, Em. He said it's the least he can do after everything he's put us through." Mia hesitates a moment. "And for what happened to Wyatt."

"Mia, I don't think Ryan and Colin can do anything for us. It's up to us to end it so everyone can move on."

"He said something else, too," Mia says with the slightest smile.

"Well?" I ask, hoping against hope that it isn't more bad news.

"He told me he loves me."

CHAPTER
9

"HE *LOVES* YOU?" I ask, barely able to get the words out of my mouth without choking.

"I guess Terra's vibration melted his hard candy shell," Mia says with a shrug. "After you left he just sat here, staring at his feet, for a long time. Long enough that I started to feel uncomfortable. When he finally looked up at me, he had tears in his eyes, and it was like he was seeing me for the first time. I started to think he'd gone crazy, but he moved toward me and got down on both knees, taking my hands in his.

"He told me he's been lost for so long. He said, 'Mia, I don't know how you found me in the dark place I've kept myself hidden, but you and your sisters—you've saved me. I hated myself, and everyone around me. You showed up right in the middle of the place I thought I'd be trapped forever. You crashed in, and forced me to look up; to face all the demons that fight for my attention. I feel like I might find my way back. Instead of the void, I see color again. Like—' " Mia pauses.

"Well?" I ask with bated breath.

" 'Like the gold flecks in your brown eyes.' "

I smile. "Nice."

Blushing, she continues. "As he said it, his face softened; all the sharp angles and angry lines melted away. He looked more like Ryan—kind and gentle.

"I was speechless, but before I could think of anything to say, he stood and pulled me up with him. He looked me in the eyes and said, 'I'm going to kiss you.' " She smiles to herself, seeming to forget I'm even there.

"*And?*" I prod.

"And, he did."

"Wha... Wow. Okay," is all I can manage at first. Mia and I stare at each other for a moment, laughter finally breaking the awkwardness. "And do you love him?" I ask.

"I don't hate him," Mia says. "I told him I'm not sure how I feel. It's weird to go from mortal enemy to love interest in a few days. Not to mention the fact that he threatened you."

"I can take care of myself, thanks," I reply, still trying to wrap my mind around Colin's 180-degree turn. "So—what now?"

"We finish what we came to do: give DéSolé the book and put an end to the drama and intrigue."

"You make it sound so easy."

Terra and the brothers come out of the house with drinking water for our trip and Ryan gets behind the wheel, starting the engine. "Ah, she's a faithful gal," he says, patting the dashboard.

"Not much to look at, though," Colin quips, holding the passenger door open for Terra.

As we pull away from the house, Rosamie waves to us from the porch. Miracle lies curled at her feet, guarding the house until we return.

Mia sits between me and Colin, and I watch Terra's hair blowing in the wind from the open passenger window. The air is cool and sweet, clearing my mind as I breathe it in.

Though the revelations of the day are still fresh in our minds, we drive toward the city in comfortable silence, the truth having found its place among us. It's so peaceful, I slow time down to savor the feeling. I inhale deeply, and as I let the air leave my lungs, I feel my own energy float free of my body. The sound of the the van engine and the wind rushing in the windows fades as Terra's hair wafts in slow motion. I feel my heart beating gently in my chest, matching the pattern of my breath, in…and out…in…and out… *thump…thump… thump*…. I feel intoxicated, as though moving through a deliciously lazy dream as we pass jade-green fields and clean sheets waving languidly while drying in the sun.

As we reach the city, I bring time back to its normal pace so we're all fully present driving into the Lower Ninth Ward. The damage from Hurricane Katrina is still painfully visible. Empty lots overgrown with grass outnumber houses on most of the blocks. Of the houses that do remain, many have boarded windows and damaged roofs. While some families returned to rebuild, many left forever, the desolation and destruction too much to overcome.

Water damage from the flooding is as high as twelve feet in some places, a terrible watermark that continually reminds everyone of Katrina's vengeance. A few small stores returned, but the rain and wind destroyed most of the businesses, the cost of starting over too far out of reach, even with the donations and FEMA money that came in. As if the storm weren't enough to break the city's heart, crooked politicians and unscrupulous contractors skimmed millions from the money that was meant for rebuilding.

Old couches and chairs still sit, unused and unclaimed, in driveways.

I think of our big house in Santa Cruz, high on a cliff, well above the waves even in the worst of storms. I try to imagine the pain of having all our possessions washed away, our home destroyed, and our family scattered far away from everything we grew up with.

Mia leans toward me, whispering in my ear, "There are people wandering everywhere, lost, and looking for their homes."

A group of children run down the cracked sidewalk, smiling and waving. Mia's eyes well up with tears as she waves at them.

The van bounces along the damaged road, potholes and wide cracks in the asphalt still waiting to be repaired.

We leave the Ward and head to the French Quarter to get lunch. While we eat, Mia calls our lawyer, Mr. Seville, asking him to research the best way to donate money to help the area rebuild. She wants the money to go where it's truly needed, not lining the pockets of yet another duplicitous predator.

As she finishes the call, Colin smiles at her.

"What?" she asks.

"You're a good person," he says quietly.

She rests her head on his shoulder. "Thank you."

It's strange seeing Colin act affectionately. It wasn't so long ago that my visions of him included his hands wrapped tightly around my throat. He did his best to scare us in his pursuit of the book, and it worked. It's taken a long time to forgive him for that. But it was desperation that drove him, making him feral; and somehow, his feelings for Mia are making him human again.

As much as I'd like to believe it can happen to anyone, I doubt we'll ever see a human side to Madame DéSolé.

Not wanting to leave Cheddar for too long, we head back to the plantation. Every few minutes, I see Ryan looking back at me in the rearview mirror. I can't read his face and wonder what he's thinking.

We arrive at Rosamie's just before sunset. Cheddar is still asleep, and after checking on him I walk Ryan and Colin back to the van. Colin gets in and shuts the door, leaving Ryan and me alone. "Em, I'm sorry about what happened to Cheddar," he says, staring down at his boots. "It's my fault."

"I don't blame you. If anyone deserves the blame, it's DéSolé Marchand. Eventually she'll pay for what she did."

"I don't want you to take any risks," Ryan says, finally looking at me.

"It seems like everything we do here is a risk," I reply. "We just want to end all of this and go home."

"Okay." He looks back down at the ground. "I know your mind is set. But before any of that, I'd like to take you to meet my grandmother."

I can tell I've hurt his feelings, making it clear I want to leave New Orleans. "I'd like to meet her," I say, hoping it lessens the sting.

He hugs me before he leaves. I manage to hug him back lightly, but my feelings are guarded. So much has changed since Halloween night.

Terra and Mia come down the front steps as the van pulls away. "Rosamie says she plans to stay in the living room with Cheddar for the night," Terra says.

We walk toward the guest cottages and find Miracle sitting in the middle of the path, staring at the trees, her tail twitching back and forth.

"They're out there again," Terra says. "DéSolé's people. I can feel them."

Before I can say anything, Mia steps off the path and walks across the property directly toward the trees. "Mia, wait!" I yell, but she continues, undaunted.

"She isn't going to stop; let's go," Terra says, grabbing my hand as we follow.

When we reach the trees, we see three of DéSolé's followers—teenage boys, dressed in the same dingy white drawstring pants and loose-fitting longsleeved shirts they seem to favor—standing just beyond the property line. They don't look much older than we are, seventeen at most, with shortly cropped hair and smooth, hairless faces. Their expressions are hard and angry in the fading light. They stand stock still, two of them staring past us. The boy in the middle, though—his eyes dart nervously from me to my sisters, finally settling on Mia.

"What do you want?" she says, walking up to the boy in the middle until they're almost nose to nose.

He smirks at her, unfazed. "It isn't what we want; it's what Madame DéSolé wants. She knows you have the conjure book and you must return it."

"We'd like nothing more," says Mia.

"She will be most pleased," he says. "Meet us tomorrow at sunset, behind the cabin where we took your friend."

The other two boys laugh.

"You can wipe the smiles off your faces," Mia says, anger rising in her voice as she points to the ground where we stand. "You can't even set foot on this land."

"Maybe not. But you'll be on our land tomorrow." The three turn to walk back into the shadows of the trees.

"We'll be there," Mia shouts as they disappear into the darkness.

We start back toward the cottage as Mia looks back over her shoulder to make sure DéSolé's messengers of doom have fully retreated. "Jackasses," she mutters, stomping as she walks ahead of me and Terra.

"They were scared," Terra calls ahead to her. "They were trying to hide it, but I could feel it!"

"Not as intimidating without their queen, are they?" I say as we try to catch up.

Mia reaches the door first and throws it open just

in time for Miracle to slip in and take her favorite spot on Mia's bed. Mia sits down next to the cat, stroking her sleek fur, but I can see the vein in her neck pulsing.

"Calm down," I say, pulling on a tank top and sweats. "You're going to give yourself a heart attack."

"I'm so over this cat-and-mouse game. No offense, Miracle." Miracle stretches out, offering her stomach. Clearly no offense has been taken.

"Okay, well, we all live to fight another day," says Terra, yawning and turning out the light. "Can we get some sleep now?"

As I try to coax myself to sleep, I can hear Mia tossing angrily in her bed. Even Miracle's charms can't soothe her after our meeting with DéSolé's emissaries.

After a night of fitful sleep, I wake feeling more exhausted than I did going to bed. I dress quickly, thinking of Rosamie's coffee, and leave the twins sleeping in the cottage.

Rosamie stands at the sink when I walk into the kitchen. Thankfully there's a full pot of coffee made. "I see you got about as much sleep as I did," she says as she surveys the dark circles under my eyes.

"How's Cheddar?" I ask, pouring myself a steaming cup.

"He's sleeping, but he does wake up long enough to eat. My soup has almost miraculous curative power, though I think he'd wake up just for chicken broth. That boy is definitely food motivated."

We sit together at the dining-room table for a while,

drinking our coffee. "We're returning the book to Madame DéSolé," I say, finally breaking the silence.

"I see," says Rose.

"And once we do, we're going home."

"And that will be that?" she asks, smiling like someone who knows better, and it drives me crazy because I know she probably does.

"I hope so," I say, letting any pretense of confidence fall away. "But before all of that happens, Ryan's taking me to meet his grandmother."

"Oh, she's a good woman," Rose says. "Wise, too. You'll do well to listen to anything she has to say."

Before I have a chance to ask what she means, Ryan walks in through the back door. "How's our boy?" he asks quietly.

"Sleeping still," says Rose. "Coffee?"

"Not today. I want to get over to Gran's."

"So I hear. You'd best let her see the book before the girls give it to DéSolé. I'd venture to guess she'll have a thing or two to say about the whole ordeal, even if it's just to wave her hand over it for good luck." Rosamie pulls the book from her robe pocket and hands it to Ryan.

"You slept with it?" I ask, raising an eyebrow.

"You said safe and sound; it couldn't be much safer than on my hip."

Before we leave, I hug Rose tightly, her strength a sure comfort in the face of the uncertain twenty-four hours looming ahead of me.

It's early enough that the streets are mostly clear as we make our way into Metairie. Stately homes, painted beige and pale yellow sit behind bright-green, manicured lawns. The neighborhood lacks the vibrant color of the French Quarter, but seems relatively untouched by the damage we saw in the Ninth Ward.

We pull up to a well-kept, two-story house with large covered porches along the bottom and top floors. Hanging flowerpots sway in the breeze and neatly planted flower beds line the front of the house. "She still does all her own gardening," Ryan says as we walk to the front door.

He rings the bell and within seconds the door opens. Standing in the doorway is a small woman, just shy of five feet tall. Her hair is snow white and her eyes sparkle behind wire-rimmed glasses perched delicately on her nose. "My sweet boy!" she says as her grandson leans down to hug her.

"Gran, this is Emerald Tempest," he says, leading me into the house.

"Oh my, aren't you a pretty thing," she says, taking both my hands in hers. "Come in, come in, I've got sweet tea and cookies in the living room."

The house is spotless, with gleaming antique furniture and shining wood floors. Fine china teacups sit evenly spaced in an armoire with paned glass doors in the main hallway. Large paintings of elegant women cover the walls.

We sit on an overstuffed couch upholstered in red velvet as Ryan's grandmother hands me a glass of iced sweet tea. "You have a beautiful home, Mrs. Laurent," I say, taking a sip.

"Thank you. I was born and raised right here in this house. Spent plenty of time along the bayou with this boy, though. Raised him up right," she says proudly, handing Ryan a plate of sugar cookies before sitting down in a matching red velvet chair. "Emerald, how is your mother?"

Suddenly I'm not thirsty, and I set my tea down. Admittedly, it's already half gone.

"I'm sorry, dear girl," Gran says. "I didn't mean to upset you. It's just that I know she's troubled. She was such a help to me when she worked here. But, as I'm sure you know, she didn't stay long."

"I know," I answer, "and I'm sorry for all the trouble she caused your family."

"No need to apologize," she assures me. "Far be it from me to judge a desperate woman, let alone her innocent kin. So long as everything's made right, we can all move on."

Ryan shifts in his seat. "Gran, I think you should tell her what you told me about Madame DéSolé."

Gran sips her tea and sets her glass down on a coaster. "Emerald, I know Eva left you and your sisters to be raised by your grandmother. Has she told you why?"

"She said she was too young; that she wasn't prepared to be a mother," I reply.

"While that may be true, there's much more to the story. You deserve to know the truth in its entirety. Your parents lived here in New Orleans before you were born. While your mother was pregnant with your sisters, your father met DéSolé Marchand. Now, when DéSolé sees something she wants for herself, she takes it. And she wanted your father for herself."

Her words hit me like ice water and I struggle to process them.

"Your mother convinced your father to move back to California, but DéSolé refused to give up," Gran continues, her eyes anything but playful now. "After you were born, your father left Eva and returned to New Orleans. It broke your mother's heart. She never recovered from it. She felt she had failed you girls by bringing you into a situation where she couldn't support you and provide you the lives you deserved. The shame she felt grew too much to bear, so she left you and your sisters with your grandmother to raise you as her own."

Everything I feel, and thought I understood, begins shifting inside me like a movable puzzle.

Gran takes a sip of her tea and gazes out the front window, clearly pained to impart such a story. It would be fascinating if it weren't my own. "Eventually, DéSolé grew tired of your father, and he left New Orleans to find Eva and try to repair things. But it was too late. You, my dear, came here to find a book that holds a secret, and great power, but not the kind that your mother or Colin sought. Your mother wanted to go back to a time where she could reverse her decision to leave you girls; Colin wanted to go back and save his own mother. These things are simply not possible, I'm afraid."

As the truth settles around me, my heart feels heavy with regret for my family—but also burns with anger at DéSolé and my father.

Gran eyes me earnestly over the rims of her glasses. "Emerald, the book belongs to you and your family alone. It was never meant to be in the hands of another. Do you understand me?"

"Yes, ma'am, I do," I say weakly. I doubt I've convinced her.

She rises from her chair, picking up the tray. "I'll freshen this up and give you two some privacy to talk."

She leaves the room as I stare ahead, unable to look at Ryan. We sit quietly for a while as I try to imagine what Mia and Terra's reactions will be. I suddenly feel a new sense of compassion for Eva, and I hope Mia will feel the same.

"I thought you should know the truth," Ryan says. "You okay?"

"Trying to be. But it's hard to accept the truth when I get a different version of it every day." The new information changes things, and will surely put Mia on the offensive when we meet DéSolé tonight.

Ryan's grandmother returns with a tray of fresh cookies. "Ma'am," I say, "tonight my sisters and I are meeting Madame DéSolé. She thinks we're giving her the book. Otherwise, I don't think she'd come."

"That's not happening," Ryan interrupts.

Irritated, I hold my hand up. "Yes, it is. Now that I know the truth, I need to confront her. She needs to understand the damage she's caused."

"She's not likely to care about that, but you girls should have your say," says Gran, offering us each a cookie before setting the tray down and carefully making her way back to her seat. Her spirit may be fierce, but her frame is slight and fragile. She takes small, measured steps and settles cautiously back into the chair. "Ryan, you need to check your worry. The bond Emerald and her sisters share has more authority than DéSolé's raggedy old self could ever hope to conjure up. Nevertheless," she adds, turning to me, "Ryan and Colin should follow you. Once DéSolé realizes you're not giving up the book, she'll pitch herself a fit."

Ryan starts to argue, but a knock at the door cuts him off. "Are you expecting someone?" he asks.

"I most certainly am not," says Gran, followed by a deep sigh. Pushing herself back to a fully standing position, she makes her way to the front door with Ryan and I close behind. She opens the door and Eva and Tyler stand before us. "Oh my goodness, come in!" Mrs. Laurent exclaims as Ryan steps out onto the porch to see if the new arrivals have been followed. Seeing no one, he steps back inside, locking the door behind him.

Eva looks rested and happy, her hair pulled back neatly into a French twist, and her silver hoop earrings sparkling brightly against her rosy cheeks.

Tyler hugs Ryan's grandmother, smiling brightly at me. "Tyler, aren't you a sight for sore eyes!" Mrs. Laurent says, hugging her back tightly. "Make yourself at home; there's sweet tea in the kitchen."

"Thanks, Gran. Ryan, will you join me?" Tyler says as she ushers Ryan away, leaving the rest of us to talk.

"Eva Tempest, it seems it's been a lifetime," says

Gran, leading her into the living room. We sit together on the couch, with Eva in the middle.

"Mom," I say gently, "I know what happened with you, dad, and Madame DéSolé. I understand why you left."

Eva sighs and straightens her shoulders. "It was a mistake, and I accept responsibility for it. I can't change the past, but I intend to make things right, starting with asking forgiveness—from you, your sisters, and Mrs. Laurent." She holds her head high, looking straight into Gran's eyes.

"Dear, sweet child," Gran says lovingly, "you've suffered enough with the past. I certainly forgive you, and in time, all your daughters will too. Now, how long will it be before you forgive yourself?"

Eva, lowering her head, replies quietly, "I don't know."

"You raise your head right back up, child," Gran says, lifting Eva's chin with a diminutive but steady hand. "You deserve forgiveness. We've all given it, and you need to give yourself the peace of an unburdened heart."

Eva turns to me. "Have you forgiven me, Emerald?"

"Of course I have," I say, hugging her. "Terra has, too. And Mia will come around; she just needs time. For now, it might be best if you lay low, stay close to Tyler, and let us sort out a few things."

Gran's eyes meet mine. She understands I don't want to tell Eva we're confronting DéSolé tonight. "You have strong, beautiful daughters, Eva. A second chance is a beautiful gift. You take it, now, and protect it."

"There's nothing I want more," Eva says as Ryan and Tyler rejoin us.

"Eva," says Ryan, "we'll drop you and Tyler off then take the book back to Rosamie's."

"That's an excellent idea," says Gran. "I'll wrap it up for safekeeping. It's done quite a bit of travelling in the past few months." She takes the book and, before leaving the room, pulls me aside. "Emerald, remember what I've told you: there's nothing DéSolé can say or do that you can't protect yourself from, as long as you and your sisters stick together."

"Always," I whisper, and hug her tightly. "Thank you."

"And don't worry about Eva," she adds with a sly smile. "No one will touch her while she's with Tyler. Tyler has charms of her own, you see—just as you and your sisters do."

I smile at her. "How long have you known?"

"Since a little before the beginning, child," says Gran Laurent with a wink before disappearing through the door.

She's back moments later and hands me the book, safely wrapped in heavy paper and tied with twine. As we leave, she waves and nods to me, as if reassuring me that I can handle everything that's coming my way tonight.

We drop Eva and Tyler off at the St. Philip, with Tyler promising to keep Eva safely in her care. As we drive back to the plantation, I watch the New Orleans landscape roll by with a new sense of connection. The city is part of my history in a way I hadn't known before today. As mixed as my feelings are, I feel I'll leave a part of myself here when I return home.

As we pull up to the main house, Ryan says, "I'll give you time to talk to Mia and Terra. Colin and I will come back to pick you up about six." Before I can shut the passenger door, he asks, "Em—are you sure you want to do this?"

"Of course I don't want to—I need to," I say firmly.

After Ryan leaves, I bring the twins out to the back of the property, hoping the bright sunshine will soften the blow as I relay the things Gran told me.

Tears are shed for both ourselves and our mother. As we talk, our mutual anger toward our father and DéSolé grows. We'll never get the time we lost back and there's no way to know how things would have turned out if Eva had stayed to raise us. What sickens me most is that the chance to find out was taken away from us by the selfishness of our father and the interference of DéSolé Marchand. The blame we previously cast solely upon our mother is now evenly spread among the three of them.

We have no plan for the evening—only the resolve to confront the woman who played such a huge role in changing the course of our lives. After tonight, my hope is that we can go home and start to put our lives back together; to try and redefine our relationship with Aracelia, and perhaps move forward with Eva. Soon enough, we'll confront our father, if for no other reason than to ask him what on earth he was thinking.

For now, we can't see beyond tonight. As the sun sinks lower, I watch Mia's anger toward our mother diminish, finding a new target in Madame DéSolé.

CHAPTER
10

THE TWINS AND I SIT IN SILENCE as we try to eat the dinner Rosamie's prepared. Mia picks at her food as Terra studies her fork between small bites. All I can do is stare at my plate.

Storm clouds gather outside and while there's no rain, thunder crackles in the distance, making the lights in the dining room flicker.

As much as I want to confront Madame DéSolé, I'd rather be home, two thousand miles away, safe and secure with my family and Cheddar.

Unable to do anything else, we clear the table and head to the cottage to change our clothes. Miracle leads the way, walking quickly. Once inside, she jumps onto Mia's bed and sits quietly, watching as we dress, her tail slowly swishing back and forth. "What's up with her?" asks Mia.

"She's picking up our vibration," Terra says as she sits next to Miracle, running her hand over the cat's sleek black fur. "She can feel the tension."

The thunder is booming above us, and just as an ear-splitting clap breaks over the cottage, green sparks of electricity flash between Miracle's fur and Terra's hand.

"Holy *crap!*" I yell, jumping backwards. "What was that?!"

"Whoa!" Mia shouts, pushing away from Miracle and Terra.

"Neat!" Terra assesses her hand for damage and, finding none, waves it over Miracle's back to see if she can recreate the sparks.

"Don't *do* that," Mia says, pulling Terra's hand away. "Are you okay?"

"I'm fine! That was awesome!"

Miracle seems to agree and purrs loudly as she pushes her head against Terra's hand.

"Okay, what just happened?" I ask as I take her hand and inspect it like a palm reader.

"It's Miracle—she's charmed! Or, more accurately, she's charged," Terra says excitedly, pulling her hand away. "The sparks were electrons discharging when I touched her. I knew it! I knew I felt her buzzing when we first got here. That means my charm is electrically based!" She paces, the gears in her head nearly smoking with how fast her thoughts are racing.

"Okay, Magneto, calm down," Mia says. "Did it hurt?"

"Not at all!"

"Then do it again," I say as the thunder continues to roll above us.

The three of us stare at each other for a moment as

Miracle rolls around in the blankets, purring louder than we've ever heard her. A wide smile crosses Terra's face as Mia pushes the blankets back, away from Miracle. Terra rubs her hands together before sitting back down on the bed.

"That's cheating," I say.

"I don't think so. It's not static. It's a reaction between me and Miracle." Terra scoots closer to Miracle and carefully reaches out to stroke her back. As if on cue, the green sparks sizzle between them like fireworks, but this time there's a pop and the lights of the cottage go out. The sparks glow green in the darkened room. Miracle twists and rolls happily under Terra's hand, clearly enjoying the interaction. "This is crazy!" Terra shrieks.

"What does it feel like?" asks Mia, her face illuminated by the eerie green glow.

"Like bees, but without the sting." Terra smiles. "I *knew* she was protecting us. She must have an electric field around her, and somehow it's keeping DéSolé away from the property. I bet the land is charged, too!"

"All right, before you run outside and start massaging the dirt, remember we have something important to do tonight," I say as Terra and Miracle release each other and the sparks abruptly stop.

Mia clicks on a flashlight, flooding the room with harsh light. "Terra, your hair," she says.

Terra's hair has gone curly and floats around her head like snakes.

"From Magneto to Medusa," I say, tossing her a scrunchie. "Stay charged up; we may need that later."

We leave the cottage to return to the main house. It's almost completely dark and Ryan and Colin will be here soon. I tuck the book under my jacket to give to Rosamie.

Just as we enter the house, lightning and thunder open the sky directly above, causing the kitchen lights to flicker and go out.

"Okay, really? How old is the wiring here?" I complain as I bump into Mia, causing her to drop the flashlight.

"Terra, can you light up your hand?" Mia asks.

"Sorry, I don't glow on demand," Terra says, picking up the flashlight so we can look for matches.

We help Rosamie light candles and hurricane lamps and stack more wood on the fire. Cheddar stirs and turns over, but doesn't wake up. It's just as well—if he knew where we were going, he'd try to come.

"He's getting stronger by the hour," says Rose. "He'll be ready to travel in a day or two."

"Thank you for everything you've done, Rose," I say, following her into the kitchen. "Would you mind doing one more thing for me?"

"Of course not. What is it?"

I hand her the book, still wrapped in the paper and twine. "Will you keep this safe while we're gone?"

Rosamie looks at the book, then at me. "You know DéSolé will be none too pleased when she finds out you aren't giving it to her."

"I doubt anything I do will please her," I say. "But she's not getting this book."

"Good on you for standing up to her," she smiles. "Remember, her particular brand of magic is nothing more than a combination of a sharp tongue and a few parlor tricks."

Just as I'm about to hand the book over, Mia and Terra join us. Mia reaches for the book, but I pull it away before she can grab it. "We're giving it to DéSolé," Mia says. "This has to end tonight!"

I shake my head, desperate to get through to her. "Mia, we can't. Ryan's grandmother says it belongs to us, and we're supposed to keep it."

Mia looks from me to our host. "Rosamie, would you mind giving us a few minutes alone?"

"Of course," Rose says, though as she returns to Cheddar, closing the living-room doors after her, her eyes betray concern.

"We're not giving it back!" I whisper to Mia.

"We are," she says, trying to grab the book from my hand. "If we don't, DéSolé will follow us home. It's nothing but trouble."

"We aren't!" I whisper back, raising my arm and holding the book high above both our heads. Being a bit taller than Mia allows me to play keepaway, much to her frustration.

"We've done what we needed to do, Em. We got the book back from Eva, and we told Colin the truth. We don't *need* it."

For a moment I shake my head just because I can't think of a response. Something about the way Ryan's grandmother insisted it belongs to us makes me think we do need it.

Before I have to come up with a counterpoint to Mia's argument, Rose pushes the kitchen door ajar. "Ladies, if you don't mind, I think I have an alternative that will buy y'all some time." With a wicked grin, she offers me a package wrapped exactly as the spell book has been wrapped, in heavy paper and twine. I take it from her and its weight is almost exactly that of the spell book.

"What is it?" I ask.

"Another book of conjures and spells. Looks close enough that, with any luck, she won't notice—until all of you are safe at home, anyway. These silly little books were popular back in the day. I don't know why she wants your particular book so badly, but you surely want to take the advice Grandma Laurent gave you. The real book must stay in your hands."

As soon as the words leave her mouth, Ryan and Colin come through the back door. Mia jumps up and tucks the decoy book into the top of her jeans, under her jacket; I hand the real book to Rosamie for safekeeping.

"You ready to do this?" Ryan asks as Colin stands silent.

"Ready as we'll never be," Mia quips.

We say goodbye to Rosamie, and the twins and I take turns kissing Cheddar on the forehead before leaving. In addition to everything else, my heart is sick with worry that he'll still be unconscious when we return. I have no doubt my sisters feel the same way.

"Don't forget to leave room for Wyatt," Mia reminds us in a whisper as we get into the van.

As the main house shrinks in the rearview and we

roll through the fields toward the gate, I notice Mia's face gradually tightening into a frown as she looks through one window and then another. "What is it?" I whisper.

"The slaves who died here before the Civil War," she says. "They're all around us. They know we're going to confront DéSolé. They're all saying *Bon chance.*"

"French for *Good luck*," I muse. "But why haven't you seen them until now?"

I can tell Mia's fighting tears as she says, "They're usually looking for their families—their wives, husbands, children, parents." I hug her and she wipes her eyes, not wanting to attract Ryan or Colin's attention. "They came back just to wish us Bon chance."

Mia looks out her window with a sad smile. "Thank you," she whispers.

I wrap her in a giant hug. What I know about slavery from history books is heartbreaking enough, but to actually look into their eyes and hear their voices like Mia can... I don't know how she bears the burden of her charm. Mia's tough exterior washes completely away when she sees and hears the people who've suffered the most.

We drive toward the swamp in silence, our moods growing heavier with the uncertainty of what's to come. As if on cue, a light drizzle begins to fall. "Of course," I say sarcastically, remembering our last trip into the swamp, soaking wet and covered in mud. I try to steel my resolve thinking about a hot, lavender-scented bath on the other side of our meeting.

We reach the boat launch as darkness overtakes

the last of the light. The landscape looks sinister, with the Spanish moss hanging like ghosts in the trees and raindrops collectively whispering on the water's black surface.

"We're going to take two boats," Ryan announces. "The three of you go ahead, and Colin and I will follow behind you a short way." After starting the engine, he shows me how to work the throttle. "Just go easy on it," he says, placing his hand over mine. "Forward to go, ease back to slow down, and right in the middle to stop—although that's neutral, and you'll probably keep moving a bit until you tie off to the dock."

Without warning, he takes my face in his hands and kisses me quickly, saying nothing as he leaves us to join Colin on the second boat.

Mia clears her throat and I realize I've forgotten to breathe while watching Ryan go. "Right," I say, joining her and Terra on our boat. I try to look focused, but can feel my cheeks burning.

"Wyatt says you need to work on your technique," Mia murmurs, and Terra makes smooching noises.

"What do you know about it, Wyatt?" I say, looking right at the bow where I know he must be perched. "Better watch out or you'll end up back in the water."

"Because you push him?" Mia giggles. "Nice threat, Miss Physics. You'll go right through him and end up in the water yourself."

Terra snorts. "Miss Physics."

Mia's smiling now, and I realize I am, too—in spite of how afraid we are; in spite of everything.

We motor toward the fishing cabin, cruising slowly with only a spotlight on our boat to light the way. Ryan and Colin follow in darkness. The water is murky and green where our beam hits it, with nothing visible beneath the surface. I see nothing beyond the banks but darkness, and the pulse in my ears beats louder than the boat engine.

We approach the cabin's decrepit dock, but I come in too fast and the side of the boat scrapes against the pilings, producing a high-pitched *screeeech*. "My bad," I grimace after killing the engine.

"Way to make a stealthy approach, Em," Mia says, hopping out to hitch the boat to the dock. Ryan and Colin wait a short distance behind in case we're being watched.

I'm certain we are.

Terra grabs a flashlight from the boat and helps me onto the dock, lighting our way to the cabin. We step carefully, listening for any sound other than our footsteps on the creaking boards and the patter of rain on foliage and water. "I can feel somebody," Terra whispers. "They're watching."

"It's all right," I say as we reach the cabin, "just keep walking."

"Which way?"

"Wyatt says there's a clearing to the left of the cabin," says Mia.

"Is there a path?" I ask.

Mia listens, then sighs. "Not so much."

We push our way through the trees and overgrowth,

trying to avoid sinking in mud or stepping on anything with scales and sharp teeth. "I see lights up ahead," Terra says.

We reach the clearing, lit by oil lanterns hung in a wide circle. I don't see anyone, but as soon as we enter the circle, I hear, "Good evening, Miss Tempest," in a low, honeyed voice. "I thank you and your lovely sisters so much for joining me."

As we turn to find the source of the voice, DéSolé Marchand emerges from the darkness. She enters the circle slowly, her lithe frame almost gliding along the ground, piercing blue eyes glowing in the lantern light. I expect to see her followers appear behind her, but she's alone.

A wide smile crosses her face as her gaze settles on me. "I see your father in you."

I feel Mia bristle beside me. "We didn't come to talk about him," I reply coldly.

DéSolé cocks her head to one side. "Oh? But he's one of my favorite subjects."

"We don't want to hear it," Mia says, stepping forward.

DéSolé, folding her arms, turns to Mia with a look of mock concern. "Don't you, though?"

I pull Mia back, stepping in front of her. "You may be part of our family's past, but you have no place in our future." Somehow I manage to sound a lot more confident than I feel.

She studies me with scorn. "Your eyes betray you, child."

I square my shoulders and step closer. "You've had no interest in our father for a very long time, but we know what you do want."

Her eyes glitter with desire. "And do you have it, clever girl?"

"We do. But before we give you the book, you have to agree to leave our family alone forever."

"A simple request," she says, uncrossing her arms and placing her hands over her heart. "You have a bargain."

I turn and nod to Mia, but as she pulls the book out from under her jacket, a voice from the darkness cries, "Mia!" Colin and Ryan step out of the dark and into the circle. "Please don't," Colin entreats her.

"The Laurent brothers," smirks DéSolé, showing no surprise. "How lovely you could come."

Mia ignores her, addressing Colin. "It doesn't matter. Nothing in this book can help you. The spells are worthless."

Colin's struggle is evident from his expression. In his eyes, I see the delusion that he can ever bring his friend back begin to crumble. "Mia...don't do this."

She shakes her head. "I care about you, Colin, but nothing is worth having this woman in our lives for another minute." She turns to DéSolé, offering her long-sought prize.

Just as DéSolé reaches out, Colin lunges for it, knocking Mia to the side, sending her and the wrapped book to the ground.

DéSolé laughs and sweeps one hand in the air. As she does, her followers dart out of the darkness all around us and pour into the circle of light, grabbing Colin and Ryan by the arms.

Picking the package up, DéSolé gently wipes the dirt from the paper and twine. "How quickly our alliances shift," she coos, gliding toward Colin and brushing his cheek with the back of her hand. "You used to be my pet; my very favorite. But now I've lost you, haven't I?" She casts a sideways glance at Mia.

Terra and I pull Mia up from the ground and stand together, shoulder to shoulder.

"Ah, the Tempest Trinity. I suppose it's three against one, then?" DéSolé gestures to her followers to back away, pulling Ryan farther from the circle.

I turn to look at Mia, and then Terra. Without saying a word, we clasp hands to merge our powers, but nothing happens. I tighten my grip on their hands, but still—nothing.

DéSolé buries her face in her hands and begins to weep, her shoulders shaking. Her weeping turns to a piercing cry. But as she lifts her face, her cries turn into wicked, uncontrollable laughter. "Your anger's distracted you. It's divided your strength. You couldn't have possibly thought your charms were enough to stop me, here, on my own land? That's right, you're standing on land that belongs to me, and your precious Miracle can't protect you here as she does on the plantation. You're powerless!"

DéSolé's laughter rises in pitch until it's a deafening scream. I feel nauseous and shut my eyes tightly, the noise so unbearable that I release Mia and Terra's hands to cover my ears.

The screaming stops, and when I open my eyes, DéSolé is moving backward, clutching the book in one arm and dragging a limp, half-conscious Colin in the other, white powder covering his face. Ryan struggles in the hold of DéSolé's followers, watching in horror as she and Colin fall backward, plunging into the deep, murky water just beyond the clearing.

"*No!*" Ryan screams as the boys holding him let him go and disappear into the woods as quickly as they emerged.

As Ryan scrambles toward the water, Mia shouts to us, "Stop him! Wyatt says he'll drown—there are too many roots and vines in the water!"

Despite our failed merge, I gather enough strength and composure to slow time, allowing Mia and Terra to catch up to Ryan and keep him from going in after his brother. He stumbles at the water's edge and sobs. Terra drops to her knees, wrapping her arms around him and rocking him gently back and forth.

Mia stands silently at the edge of the circle, staring into the water.

I bring time back to its usual pace and sit down, exhausted, next to Terra and Ryan. Terra stands to join Mia, but as I try to take her place beside Ryan, he pushes me away. "Don't touch me."

I sit in shock for a moment, but before I can say anything, Rosamie and Cheddar walk into the circle.

Terra runs to Cheddar, hugging him tightly.

"Your friend here finally woke up," Rosamie says, pulling me to my feet. Her expression is more serious than I've ever seen it. "When I told him where you all were, I couldn't stop him from coming. From the look of things, we didn't get here fast enough. You all right?"

"I think so," I pant, unsure of anything I'm feeling.

Rose helps Ryan to his feet while Cheddar checks on Mia. "We need to get out of here and back to the house," Rose says, wrapping a blanket around Ryan as we walk back to the boat.

Cheddar helps everyone aboard the boats and unties us from the dock. As the engine comes to life, I push the throttle forward, wanting to get my sisters and myself as far away from this place as possible. Rosamie pulls ahead in the second boat with Ryan and Cheddar, motioning me to follow. I realize I have no idea how to find my way back to the parking lot. I'm grateful for Rose's presence of mind.

Flashing blue and red lights reflect on the dark water as we reach the boat launch. A bright spotlight hits the bow of Rosamie's boat.

"Ambrose Landry?" she shouts. "Is that you?"

"Yes ma'am," the officer calls back. "Got here as quick as I could."

"And I thank you for that, but can you lower the light a bit? You're just about to blind us all."

"Yes ma'am," he says, redirecting the beam onto the dock.

As we reach the dock and tie off, the young officer helps Ryan out of Rose's boat. "What the hell happened out there?" he asks, surveying us.

"It was DéSolé Marchand, and we have witnesses,"

Rosamie says, nodding toward the twins and me. "She blew that conjure powder into Colin Laurent's face and took him into the water, under the tangle of vines. It was too dangerous to go in after him."

Ambrose frowns, alarmed. "How long ago?"

"Too long, I'm afraid," she says gravely. "Ten minutes at least."

"And you girls saw her do this?" he asks me directly.

I look to Ryan but he's sitting on the dock, slumped over, with his arms wrapped around his knees. "Yes, we did," I say.

Officer Landry takes a deep breath, whistling slowly as he exhales. "I'll get the night-shift boys out looking for them. We'll send the tour-boat guides in at sunrise to recover…well, to see what we can find," he says. Leaning in, he adds in a whisper, "That's gonna be a murder charge if we can find him."

Rose whispers back, "You'd better find him. We've been through enough, and the family will want closure and justice. We are due that, certainly."

It's after midnight when we arrive back at the plantation. Ryan says nothing as Rose helps him to an upstairs bedroom. The twins and I collapse onto the couches in the living room while Cheddar makes a fire for us.

"Thank you for coming for us," Terra says.

"Just wish I'd gotten there sooner," says Cheddar, the flames illuminating his face from the side. I can read the pain and self-recrimination in his eyes.

"Even if you had," she says, "I don't think anything

would have stopped her and Colin from going into the water."

We sit quietly, listening to the crackle of firewood.

"Cheddar, you need to know something about the three of us," I say quietly. After everything we've been through, he deserves to know the truth.

"You mean about your charms?" he says, looking down at his hands.

I exchange a look of astonishment with the girls. Mia's the first of us to recover the power of speech. "You know?"

"Your grandma told me before we came here. But she made me promise not to tell you I knew unless something bad happened, and I think we've met that criterion." He takes a seat next to me on the couch as Miracle jumps up into his lap, pawing at his arm. "She thought the only way I could truly protect you was to have the full story. But I failed anyway."

"You didn't," I say. "You've been the best friend we could hope for. You've done everything in your power to keep us safe. If anyone failed us, it was our father."

"And he might not have," Mia says, "if it weren't for DéSolé Marchand."

"She's been out to hurt you all from the start," says Cheddar. "But hopefully she got what she deserved tonight. The world won't miss a person like her."

"She isn't dead," Mia says solemnly. "Only Colin."

CHAPTER

11

Miracle, Unfazed By The Revelation of DéSolé's escape, is the only one to sleep peacefully the first few nights after Colin's death. Mia sleeps fitfully the first two nights, but on the third she spends the entire night sitting by the window of the guest cottage, staring out into the darkness. I toss and turn, in and out of sleep, occasionally waking to hear Mia talking softly to someone I can't see or hear.

As the sun rises, she joins me in bed, nudging me over and pulling the quilt over our heads.

"Was it Colin?" I ask, fairly sure I already know the answer.

"He apologized for everything," she says softly, trying not to wake Terra. "He knows he frightened us, but he said he wanted so badly to help Wyatt, he couldn't see anything beyond trying to save him."

"Is he going to be okay—you know—on the other side?"

"I think so. He waited in the swamp until the police found his body, but he's with Wyatt now." She smiles. "I told him we forgive him and he should move on to find his mother. Wyatt said it would be fun to hang around and harass us, so we shouldn't get too comfortable without him."

"Great," I say, rolling my eyes.

A soft knock at the door wakes Terra. She opens the door to Cheddar holding a tray of coffees and sweet rolls. "Oh, we've missed this," Terra says, taking a cup and ushering him in.

"No trace of DéSolé, but the police recovered Colin's body," Cheddar tells us solemnly. "The cousins are having a funeral parade for him in the French Quarter this afternoon."

I look down. "I think Ryan blames me for what happened. But we can't leave New Orleans without paying our respects—especially to his grandmother." The idea of seeing Ryan makes my stomach hurt. Whether he blames me or not, he'll always associate me with the night his brother died.

Cheddar gives me an understanding shoulder-squeeze and walks out to let us dress and pack our things.

Miracle curls up in Mia's suitcase, clearly not wanting her to leave. "You need to stay here and take care of Rosamie," Mia says, scratching her head and carefully lifting her out. She follows us outside, into the bright morning sun. Although DéSolé is out there somewhere, everything around us feels lighter.

We join Rosamie in the kitchen. She's been up all

night, making food for after the parade. "Do you ever sleep?" I ask as she places sandwiches on a platter.

"Staying busy keeps my mind off things I'd rather not think about," she answers.

"I'm sorry. I didn't mean—"

"No," she interrupts. "I didn't mean you. You carry no blame for any of this." She wraps her arms around me, hugging me close. "Colin's choices put him where he is, but I'm sure he understands things clearly now—and, hopefully, he's found peace."

"Is Ryan coming to pick us up?" I ask.

She looks down before answering. "No. We'll drive into the city and meet the family at the parade. Emerald, he will get through this."

I stretch plastic wrap over the tray of sandwiches. "We'll see."

We help Rosamie arrange the rest of the food. As she and Cheddar load the trays into her truck, I take a last walk around the property. I'm grateful for the clear sky as the sun warms the grass and flowers, releasing their perfume into the air. Although I'll miss the scent, I can't wait to be home and breathe in the salty coastal air. As beautiful as it is here, I'm homesick and look forward to boarding the plane to go home.

I meet Mia and Terra on the path back to the cottage, each of them carrying clothes and hats Rosamie lent us to wear in the parade. We change inside, Mia and Terra wearing matching black pencil dresses and pillbox hats, their hair pulled back in ponytails. I slip into a midnight-blue dress and brush my hair into a French twist, fastening a matching blue silk rose on one side.

"Wyatt says, 'Unfortunate occasion, but stunning clothes,' " Mia announces, pinning her hat in place.

"Thank you, Wyatt," Terra replies loudly, right next to my ear.

"Really?" I say as we leave the cottage.

Cheddar and Rosamie are waiting for us in front of the main house.

"You ready?" he asks, standing proudly in a black suit, crisp white shirt, and black tie.

"Ready as we'll ever be," I answer, climbing into the truck.

"I'll be walking in front of the parade with the family," says Rose as she smoothes the pleats of her dark purple dress, a single strand of pearls around her neck. "You four will walk with the second line. We'll meet up with you at Grandma Laurent's house."

"Are you sure we should go there?" I ask. Giving her our condolences at the parade is one thing, but I doubt she would want us as guests.

"I most certainly am." Rose shoulders her purse and opens the door. "Their grandmother specifically invited you."

We reach the city at noon, and mourners are already gathered on Conti Street. Several women in brightly colored dresses and hats fan themselves as others twirl parasols above their heads. A brass band warms up near a mule-drawn carriage with a black casket covered in white roses. As Rosamie joins them, I see Ryan, dressed in a black suit with a black-and-gold sash across his chest.

He looks toward us but, without smiling or waving, goes back to talking with his grandmother.

Mia smiles and lifts her arm to wave.

"What are you doing?" I ask, mortified.

"It's Colin and his mother. They're together at the front of the carriage. She looks so happy."

I sigh with relief as the band begins playing a slow march. The family starts walking, and the mule pulls the carriage into motion. The women around us start singing "Just a Closer Walk with Thee" and the band's march becomes a gospel accompaniment as we make our way along the parade route. After several blocks, the music turns up-tempo and the crowd begins to dance along the street.

The bass drum beats loudly as the trombone and trumpet players turn a corner toward the cemetery. They stop marching but continue to play as the carriage enters the cemetery gates, followed by the family. I smile as I realize they're burying Colin with his mother.

The rest of the mourners continue to dance and wave goodbye as the family disappears behind the standing tombs.

The thought of Colin spending his entire life hurting and angry puts a lump in my throat. He was a little boy once, loved and cherished. It was the pain of never knowing his mother that saw him forfeit his innocence. Family and friends gathering to celebrate his life means all was not lost. I'd like to think Mia would have helped him all the way back, if they'd had the opportunity.

"Can I take off this tie?" Cheddar asks, pulling me out of my reverie. Sweat pours down the sides of his face.

"Maybe just loosen it," Terra says, blotting his face with a napkin. "We still have to go to Grandma Laurent's house."

The band keeps playing as people begin to disperse. For a moment, I think I catch sight of a familiar figure among the hedges—tall and thin, dressed entirely in black, with a thick lace veil covering her face.

Mia calls to get my attention as she, Cheddar, and Terra begin walking back to the truck. "Right behind you," I call over my shoulder.

When I look back to the hedges, the figure is gone—if I saw it at all.

On the way to Mrs. Laurent's house, Cheddar insists we stop at Café du Monde for refreshments. When he joins us at our table outside under the green-and-white awning, he's got several waters and a large order of beignets.

"You know there's going to be food at Mrs. Laurent's house, right?" asks Mia.

"Yes, but there won't be genuine New Orleans beignets in Santa Cruz; this is my last chance," he says through a mouthful of fried pastry as powdered sugar dusts his suit.

As we sit in the shade, waiting for Cheddar to destroy the evidence, another brass band begins playing in the square across the street. I think about our first day, dancing there with Ryan, and how innocent everything felt. It's clear from the way Ryan looked at me earlier that things have changed. Even if our relationship is over, I can't imagine not returning here one day. New Orleans has taken a piece of my heart, and given me a part of its own in return.

"How about we get you some sandwiches to wash those down," Mia says to Cheddar, who pours some water over his head as we walk toward the truck. He might miss the food, but he won't miss the heat.

We drive toward Metairie, leaving the French Quarter, but not my memories, behind.

People are already gathered as we reach Mrs. Laurent's house. To Cheddar's relief, the men outside have already removed their ties and jackets. "Get this thing off me," he chokes, pointing to his tie with one hand as he removes his jacket with the other. Terra loosens his tie and slides it off his neck. "No one else can die or get married, ever," he sighs. "I'm not dressing like this again."

As we walk into the house, the jovial chatter stops abruptly. Several family members look at Ryan, who gets up from the couch and leaves the living room.

"Okay, this isn't awkward at all," Mia whispers.

I'm relieved to see a friendly face in Tyler, who arranges food on a table in the dining room.

As soon as Mrs. Laurent sees us, she jumps up, exclaiming, "Oh, I'm so pleased you've come!"

The family goes back to chatting as Cheddar and the twins join Tyler at the buffet table. "I see we weren't your first stop after the parade," Tyler says, winking as she brushes a trace of powdered sugar from Cheddar's collar.

"Come, sit with me," says Mrs. Laurent as she guides me to the couch, the rest of the guests leaving us in privacy.

"Mrs. Laurent, I'm so sorry for your loss," I say earnestly.

"Thank you, child," she says, taking my hand. "But I don't think Colin had a moment of peace from the day he was born. I'm certain he's found that peace now, along with his mother, God rest their souls."

At a loss for words, all I can do is smile.

"What are your plans?" she asks.

"We fly home tomorrow. Then it's back to school, I suppose."

"So soon? I've just met you and you're already leaving! I'm sure your grandmother misses you, though, as much as we're all going to miss you when you've gone."

"Well, not all of you," I say, looking down at my lap.

"Oh, now, don't talk like that," she says reassuringly. "My grandson is just grieving for his brother. It has nothing to do with you. When he comes to his senses, he'll realize it."

I shrug slightly, thinking of nothing to say. Whether Ryan ever talks to me again or not, I have to get back to my own life.

"Tyler and I will look after your mother for you. You're family now, Emerald," Gran says as Rosamie joins us in the living room.

"We should get going—you all need a good night's

sleep before your flight tomorrow," Rose says as Gran rises to hug her. We say our goodbyes and walk out the door, no Ryan in sight.

The ride back to the plantation is peaceful, with Mia and Terra chatting happily in the back of the truck. Cheddar drives, with me squeezed between him and Rosamie.

"Well, look who we have here," Cheddar says as we pull into the driveway. I look up to see Eva sitting on the front steps of the house. Cheddar pulls to a stop, and without saying a word, Mia gets out of the truck and walks straight toward her.

Not knowing what to expect, the rest of us stay in our seats.

Eva stands up slowly. As soon as Mia reaches her, she wraps her arms around Eva, holding her close as they both begin to cry.

After a few moments, Rosamie takes the lead and gets out of the truck. Terra, Cheddar and I follow behind her. "Ms. Tempest, won't you come in?" Rose asks gently.

"I'd like that very much," Eva says, smiling tearfully at Mia.

The two of them talk privately until dinner, taking the first steps toward restoring their relationship. We spend the rest of the evening sharing stories and laughter. With thoughts of Ryan and Colin pushed out of my mind, I bask in the happy warmth of my mother and sisters being together. We have a long way to go, but it's an excellent start.

After more hugs, tears, and promises to keep in

touch, Cheddar drives Eva back into the city while the twins and I finish the last of our packing.

Once we've crawled into our beds, Miracle curls up for her last night tucked safely behind Mia's legs. "You think Mama will let us get a cat?" Mia asks sleepily.

"I think we need three," Terra says right before drifting off.

"One for each of us," I agree, more than ready to join her. But my eyes snap open and I look over to Mia. "What did you call her?"

"Who—Aracelia? I called her Mama, like we've done our whole lives. Is there a problem with that?"

In the darkness, I smirk at her comment. I'm also smiling from ear to ear. Looks like we're all calling Mama Mama again. I guess Eva, our biological mom, put in a good word for her.

I sleep deeply, dreaming of home.

It's still dark when Rosamie knocks on our door to wake us. I'm so excited to go home I dress in record time and pull my hair into a haphazard ponytail. Cheddar helps us carry our bags out to a waiting taxi while the twins and I join Rose in the kitchen for one last cup of her coffee.

"We haven't had this much adventure around here in a very long time," she says with a bittersweet smile as we stand together, sipping our coffee. "Truth be told, I'm going to miss you girls." Mia and Terra still seem half asleep, but manage smiles over their coffee mugs.

"Thank you for everything, Rose," I say, setting my cup down to hug her.

Miracle rubs against our legs, meowing in protest. "Oh no, old cat, you're staying here with me," Rose scolds, picking Miracle up and cradling her in her arms. "That's what I thought," she says as Miracle purrs contentedly. "Setting foot on this property without Miracle's approval can be, well—electrifying," she adds with a mischievous smile.

"How does she do it?" Terra asks, reaching out to pet Miracle, igniting green sparks that light up the darkened kitchen.

"Miracle comes from a long line of protective felines. I'm sure if she could talk, she'd tell you she was Egyptian royalty, descended from Bastet herself. But, honestly, she just knows her own power and wields it well. Much like you girls will learn to do."

Mia and Terra take turns hugging Rosamie and saying goodbye to Miracle before we make our way down the front steps to the taxi. As we pull away, Rose smiles and waves from the porch.

The sun is just starting to rise as we reach the airport. The taxi parks at the curb, and as we pull our baggage out of the trunk, Mia grabs my arm.

"What is it?" I ask, handing Cheddar a suitcase.

"Look," Mia says, pointing to the doors of the terminal.

There, standing alone, is Ryan. He's wearing his black leather jacket with his hands shoved into the pockets of his jeans.

"I knew it!" chirps Terra.

"Oh, you did not," Mia says, laughing.

Ryan walks toward us, looking totally unsure of himself.

"Hey, man," says Cheddar. "Glad I got to see you before we left."

"Yeah, me too," Ryan says, shaking his hand.

"We'll leave you two to talk," Mia says, grabbing a rolling suitcase and pulling Terra away with her.

"Hey," he says once they've gone.

"Hey," I answer, having no idea where this intriguing conversation is leading.

"Emerald, I didn't mean to hurt you, I just…I just don't know how I feel about anything right now," he says, eyes firmly on his boots.

"It's okay, I get it," I say. "I don't feel the same way I did when we got here."

He finally looks at me. "You don't?"

"Well, you know—so much has happened."

"Yeah," he says, looking down again.

We stand in agonizing silence as he shifts his weight back and forth.

Mia waves me toward the terminal doors.

"Ryan, I have to go," I say finally.

"I know," he says as he takes my carry-on bag. "At least let me help you with this."

I look to Mia, who gestures impatiently for me to get a move on.

"I can handle it myself, thanks." Turning back to Ryan, I take it back.

"I know, I just wanted to—"

"Don't," I say, setting the bag down on its rollers and extending the handle.

He looks at me for a moment, searching my eyes. Without saying anything further, he turns and walks away.

I walk toward the terminal, not even turning to see if Ryan looks back. All I can think about is Santa Cruz and getting my life back to normal.

"That's my girl," Mia says as I join the rest of our group at the security check.

Before boarding the plane, we stock up on snacks. Some things never change and we're not about to leave Cheddar with only airline pretzels on a five-hour flight.

As we take our seats on the plane, Cheddar leans over to Terra. "I need you to put me to sleep."

"I'm not your personal sleeping pill," she replies.

"Yeah, you are," Cheddar smiles. Now that he knows about our charms—or rather, now that we know that he knows—he's going to be impossible to live with.

As the plane takes off, I watch the city below us grow smaller and smaller.

I fall asleep before we hit 30,000 feet, dreaming of the ocean and the smell of cotton candy.

CHAPTER
12

THERE'S A FEELING OF RELIEF driving over Highway 17 toward Santa Cruz. Cresting the summit and seeing the mountains and blue-gray ocean in the distance is like taking off a heavy coat. The tightness I've felt in my chest for days eases as the scent of redwood trees blows in through the truck's open windows.

Our homecoming is far less contentious than our departure was. Mia's heart has softened, her reunion with Mama another step toward putting our family, and our lives, back together. We spend our first few days back getting to know the big house on West Cliff Drive again, basking in the delicious smells of Mama's cooking and enjoying the sound of Cheddar tinkering in the garage.

Waking up in my own bed, hearing the sound of the waves through my window, and spending hours curled up under a blanket in the library help to fade the less pleasant memories of New Orleans.

Best of all, we finally return to our favorite beach. Every place in the world has its own energy, its own unique signature. Santa Cruz is home, but it's also a consistently entertaining mix of surfers, artists, and exotic characters. I've never felt like I belonged anywhere else.

Walking down West Cliff, toward Cowell's beach, we're back to normal: shorts and flip-flops, towels over our shoulders, and Mia and Terra squabbling over the best pair of sunglasses.

The early November sky is clear and the breeze is warm. Standing at the entrance to the beach, I take in the view. Kids play in the surf, tourists walk along the wharf, and surfers carry their boards out to ride the waves at Steamer Lane just below the lighthouse. Stepping onto the sand is heavenly.

We take our usual spot, and after spreading out our towels, I lie back, taking a deep breath of fresh air.

"Do you think you'll ever talk to Ryan again?" Mia asks, adjusting her sunglasses. She won the fight for the Ray-Bans this time.

"I don't know. But if not, I'm okay with it," I reply, sitting up. "I've got you two troublemakers, and look at all those surfers out there. They have an intriguing lack of drama in their lives. I'm kind of over the emotional rollercoaster."

It's true; I am. Having a boyfriend is complicated. It's like playing a game where the rules keep changing. I'm still figuring out my own rules, and trying to navigate life with the added responsibility of another person's feelings is more of a burden than I want to carry.

"Maybe—but I don't know how any boy will ever live up to Ryan Laurent's magic," Mia laughs.

"I've had enough magic, thanks," I say, lying back down.

The memories I'll keep safely tucked in my heart are those of beginnings: the instant connection I felt seeing Ryan for the first time, the sound of his voice, and the electric excitement of getting to know him. Looking back on any experience in life, it's the sweet newness that makes us wish we could relive it. But time is moving forward now, and I have no desire to slow it down or speed it up. I just want to live in the precious now.

Ryan will work through the maze of feelings surrounding Colin's death, and Miracle will keep a close, green-eyed watch over Rosamie. The dark thought of DéSolé realizing she has the wrong book crosses my mind, but I push it away by taking a deep breath of salty sea air.

Going back to school and work, with only my sisters to keep track of, sounds like a vacation compared to the last several months. I look forward to coming home smelling of chocolate after working a shift at Martini's, and laughing at Terra when she comes home from Woodrow's smelling like fried fish. Mia will go back to work for Mr. Seville, and Cheddar, other than trying to get us to use our charms for his own gain, will go back to being Cheddar, taking care of Mama and watching out for us. It all sounds deliciously normal.

One of Terra's many admirers, a boy whose name I can't remember, walks up to us, blocking the sun. "Where have you girls been all break?"

"Hey, Matt," Terra says. "Just getting into trouble as usual."

"That sounds about right. Name's Mike, by the way."

We're off to a great start.

"Sorry," Terra says, sitting up and pushing her sunglasses to the top of her head. "The sun was in my eyes."

"Nice recovery," says Mia.

"There's a bonfire at Seabright tonight," says M-guy. "You guys should come."

"Sounds great," Mia and Terra say in unison. "Sorry again," Terra adds.

Mike smiles. "Just be there, eight o'clock."

We lie on the beach until the shadows from the cliffs stretch out long across the sand, then gather our towels and head back to the house.

During dinner, Cheddar only eats a single plate of food before clearing his dishes, kissing Mama on the cheek, and disappearing into the garage.

After finishing my own food, I go out to check on him. Expecting to find him under the hood of a car, I'm surprised to see him lying on his back on a weight bench, pressing a barbell laden with weights into the air. "What's going on out here?" I ask.

He sets the barbell onto its rack and sits up. "I realized something while I was recovering in New Orleans."

"Which was?"

"I need to be able to count on myself. I let you and your sisters down when that Marchand woman got the better of me."

I sit down next to him on the weight bench. "We don't see it that way."

"Emerald, everyone has a 'thing.' Since I've known you and your sisters, my thing has been taking care of you. In order to do that, I have to take care of myself. I have to be able to trust myself to make quick decisions."

I think about our failure to merge in the swamp and how it enabled DéSolé to take Colin's life and make her eventual escape. Just as Cheddar has decided to build his physical and mental strength, I know my sisters and I need to work on strengthening our powers. It's imperative that we're able protect everything and everyone that matters to us, including Cheddar.

"I get it," I say. "The twins and I kind of blew it in the swamp too, you know. We tried to merge our powers and we failed. And because of that, I think Ryan blames me for Colin's death."

"You're taking on a lot of responsibility for a problem you didn't create." Cheddar leans back on the weight bench and grips the barbell. "The only one to blame for any of this is DéSolé Marchand. You know it, I know it, and Ryan will figure it out," he says through gritted teeth, exhaling forcefully with every lift of the barbell.

It's funny to watch Cheddar lift so much weight, and so seriously. I'm used to watching him lift pizza to his face. His determination is inspiring, and a little unsettling. We're all in for some drastic changes for the better, it seems. "Okay, Beach Body, I'm going upstairs to change. Enjoy your workout."

"Yep," is all Cheddar can manage as I close the garage door behind me.

I head for the stairs, but just as I hit the bottom step, the doorbell rings.

"Who's at the door?" Mama yells from the kitchen over the clatter of dishes being washed.

"I'm not psychic, Mama, I'll let you know after I open it!" I call back as I turn the handle and pull open the door.

A young man with the clearest and brightest blue eyes I've ever seen stands on the porch. His freshly pressed suit and tie make it seem unlikely he's a surfer looking to park his car in our driveway. "Miss Tempest?" he asks in a tone that for some reason makes me feel like I'm in trouble.

"That's me," I answer cautiously.

With a slight smile he asks, "Would you be Mia, Terra, or Emerald?"

I step out onto the porch. "Who's asking, and what are you selling?"

"Oh, sorry," he says, reaching into an inside jacket pocket and handing me a card. "I'm not selling anything. Detective Nicholas Landry. I'm investigating the deaths of Wyatt Breslin and Colin Laurent."

I look at his card, and back at his face. The card says detective, but his face says senior in high school. "How old are you?" I blurt without thinking.

He laughs slightly. "I'm not sure that's relevant to my investigation, but I'm 22."

Before I get myself any deeper into the hole I'm digging, I stumble over an apology. "I'm sorry, you just look really young to be, you know, a—"

"An officer of the law?" He smiles. "I'm an overachiever. Do you mind if I come in?"

"Oh—right, of course," I say, ushering him into the foyer and motioning to the living room. "Have a seat; I'll get my sisters."

"Thank you. I won't take much of your time." He walks toward the couch, but doesn't sit. Putting his hands in his pants pockets, he looks around the room as though memorizing every inch.

I'm still standing in the foyer watching him when he looks back at me. "Oh, my sisters. Right," I say, silently praying to be abducted by aliens or vaporized by laser beams as I bound up the staircase two steps at a time.

When I burst into the twin's bedroom, Mia sits on the floor between their beds as she and Terra sort through a pile of clothes Terra's amassed on top of her comforter. They both stare at me while I try to form a sentence and catch my breath at the same time.

"Detective, downstairs—has questions—cute," I spit out.

"Then I'm guilty as charged," Terra says, jumping off the bed as Mia scrambles to beat her downstairs.

The three of us run downstairs and barge into the living room, only to find it empty.

"We're in the kitchen," Mama yells.

"That didn't take long," Mia sighs.

True to form, Mama has Det. Landry sitting at the table with a cup of coffee and cookies when the twins and I file in to join them. Mama lifts an eyebrow at me, and I know she's got us figured out.

"Well," the detective says as he dusts the cookie crumbs from his hands and stands to greet my sisters, "now I know who Mia and Terra are. I'm Nicholas Landry."

"Landry?" Mia asks as he shakes her hand. "Are you related to Ambrose?"

"Second cousins. A whole lot of Landrys have badges in New Orleans." He looks at Mia for what seems like a few seconds longer than necessary. "The reason I'm here is to get the details of Colin Laurent's death, any information that might tie his death to Wyatt Breslin's, and to determine the whereabouts of DéSolé Marchand."

"You came all the way here just for that? You could have called us," Terra says, prompting Mia to kick her under the table.

"That is true. However, Ms. Marchand has disappeared and she may be here in Santa Cruz."

Terra kicks back at Mia under the table.

"Why would she be here?" I ask, my stomach twisting into knots.

"That's what I hope to find out. The information I've gathered so far suggests she's looking for something your family may have. Her record, and suspected activities, put you all in a precarious position. I'd like to get to her before she gets to you," he explains, looking at Mia.

"Nothing's going to happen to them," Cheddar says as he walks into the kitchen, sweaty and red-faced.

"And you are?" Det. Landry asks as he rises to shake Cheddar's hand.

"Chet Dwyer," Cheddar answers.

"We all call him Cheddar," adds Terra.

"You can call me Chet," he says, unsmiling, as he releases the detective's hand.

"How about I do you one better and call you Mr. Dwyer?"

Mia and Terra start to laugh at the sound of "Mr. Dwyer," but then stop as abruptly as they started as Cheddar clears his throat and crosses his arms across his chest.

"If you three don't mind," the detective says, turning to my sisters and me, "I'd like to take formal statements from you tomorrow morning. For now, I think it's best that you stay close to home."

"Oh, no. Bonfire. Tonight," Mia says.

Mama immediately responds in Spanish, the gist being that there is no way on God's green earth we're going out tonight.

"*Creo que es mejor,*" Det. Landry replies.

The twins and I sit dumbstruck as Mama, grinning from ear to ear, looks from him to us. "He thinks it's best," she says, laughing, as she pushes her chair back from the table to freshen his coffee.

"No, thank you, Mrs. Tempest," he says before she can pour. "I'll be back in the morning to take the girls' statements, if that's all right."

"Of course," Mama says with a wry smile.

"Girls," the detective says, nodding in our direction as Mama escorts him to the front door.

As soon as they're out of earshot, Terra's the first to say anything. "Okay: good-looking, has a badge, and he's bilingual."

"How old is he?" Mia asks, trying and failing miserably at sounding nonchalant.

"Twenty-two. And he'll be back in the morning," I singsong.

Since we're on lockdown for the night, I might as well finally unpack my things. I've been so happy to be home, I completely forgot about the clothes I brought back. I'm sure the smell is amazing and a wash cycle in hot water is in order.

I follow the twins back upstairs and leave them giggling and whispering in their room, no doubt about the surprise visit from Detective Dreamy.

In my own room, I lock the window and close the drapes. No need to put myself on display if there's any chance DéSolé really is in Santa Cruz.

I unzip my carry-on suitcase and dump the contents on my bed. As I do, an envelope falls out of the side pocket and onto the floor.

I pick it up carefully and sit down on the side of my bed. Turning it over in my hands, I open it and unfold a sheet of notepaper, written in Grandma Laurent's measured handwriting, with a smaller piece of parchment folded inside:

Dearest Emerald,

I hope this letter finds you safely home with your sisters and grandmother. It was such a pleasure to meet you, and I see why Ryan is so taken with you.

While I hope you are settling back into life, there is a truth that must be told. Before I wrapped the spell book and gave it back to you, I removed the enclosed map from the binding. I feared you might give in to DéSolé and return the book to her.

I'm proud to know that you proved my fears to be unfounded. As a precaution, I asked Ryan to hold on to the map and return it to you once you were at the airport.

DéSolé wants only the map and what it points to—something very precious and valuable. When she finds it missing, she'll most certainly be furious. It's up to you to release the grip DéSolé has on your family and end her part in the story forever. This map is the next chapter in yours.

Be strong, and be brave, when you see her again.
Sincerely,
Josephine (Gran) Laurent

I think back to my last moments with Ryan before boarding the plane. Did he come along to say goodbye, or for the sole purpose of delivering the note? Did he even know what was inside?

As I unfold the parchment, it's clear our homecoming will be short-lived. Scanning the map, I see a familiar island, and an X several miles east of the shore. No land mass near it, just an X marking a spot in the water.

We're going to Kauai.

TO BE CONTINUED

Acknowledgments

I continue to be grateful to my friend and creative partner, Steve Hedges, for his unwavering support of the Tempest Trinity Trilogy and of my efforts to build a life around writing. I thank my team: editor John Hart, graphic designer Lindsay Gatz of vonRocko Design, and Bryan Tomasovich of The Publishing World. Without these three extraordinarily gifted people, my dream of writing books would have stayed just that, a dream.

Thanks to Santiago Scully for making the nine to five grind seem like a creative retreat.

Thanks to my youngest child, and last related roommate, Mason, for enduring my weirdness when writing. He said, "You really need to get out of the house and, you know, interact with people," only a handful of times. To my other children: Michelle, Tony, and Cara—I love you all so much. Thanks to the Hardwick and Turley families for acting as cheerleaders and advanced readers. Love and gratitude to Paul and Emily Cato, and Kathie and Bob Paradise for being there for me more times than I can count.

To my extended family, friends, and fans: thank you for buying my books, reading and recommending them, and for all the love on social media and, of course, in real life. I truly appreciate you all. On to book three....

Author Bio

Leslie shares a home in the Santa Cruz mountains with her three dogs, one cat, and a hamster named Jack White. A self-confessed Nerd Girl, she was over the moon to be able to edit much of her most recent book in an office across Highway 101 from NASA's Ames Research Center in Mountain View, CA.

More at lesliecalderoni.com

60912452R00120

Made in the USA
Charleston, SC
08 September 2016